Praying Town

An epic story of forgotten Native American
and Colonial history

Dear Steve,
Hope you enjoy the trip back in
Time. You are a true friend.
♡ Lisbeth
'Gawenase'
Johnson

L. Gawenase Johnson

Praying Town

An epic story of forgotten Native American
and Colonial history

L. Gawenase Johnson

Heart Ally Books
Camano Island, WA

Regional Map created by Aaron "Taldoz" Matney - Fiverr.
Namasket Map created by Gawenase.
Hurit created by Kathy Reed via Pixabay.

Cover photograph by Kristen Ellinger.
Cover artifacts:
    Medallion made by Cousin Dave Silversmith -
       cousindavesilversmith.com
    Leather pouch made by Roger Johnson.
    Wampum belts and wool strap woven by L. Gawenase Johnson.

Published by:
Heart Ally Books
26910 92nd Ave NW C5-406, Stanwood, WA 98292
Published on Camano Island, WA, USA
www.heartallybooks.com

ISBN-13: (epub) 978-1-63107-023-5
ISBN-13: (paperback) 978-1-63107-022-8
Library of Congress Control Number: 2018938597

1 2 3 4 5 6 7 8 9 10

❦Dedication❦

I dedicate *Praying Town* to today's Praying Indians.

They have made reprints of John Eliot's original Algonquin translation of the New Testament, descriptive linguistics books, and other writings.

Also to all of our Dawnland tribes who have persevered through four hundred years since colonization and still maintained the culture and language. No doubt, they will continue to do so for the many generations yet to come.

ᵃ᷅Table of Contentsᴮᵃ

Foreword

🌿 Praying Towns 🌿

By the year 1671, Praying Towns existed throughout the Dawnland tribes including the Wampanoag, who had welcomed the Pilgrims.

Many Wampanoag accepted Christianity and began to establish themselves in permanent communities known as Praying Towns. They were placed under the protective supervision of the Colonial government and no longer paid tribute to King Philip, the leader of Wampanoag, who continued to live in the traditional nomadic way.

Praying Towns established within the Plymouth Colony were: Meeshawn, Potanumaquut, Manamoyik, Sawkattukett, Nobsquassit, Matakees, Weeqakut, Aatuit, Pawpoesit, Mashpee, Wakoquet, Codtaninut, Ashimuit, Weesquobs, Pispogutt, Wawayontat, Sokones, Cotuhkikut, and Namasket/Middlebourough.

Damaris and Amie lived in the Praying Town of Namasket.

Preface

❦A Forgotten History Lives Again❦

I believe Lisbeth's book will be an affirmation to Native American peoples, finally bringing a little-known but significant piece of their history to light, and a revelation to others who are not so familiar with that history. Based on actual historical documents, including the journal of an eyewitness, the book plants you firmly in the experience of both Natives and European settlers in what we now know as New England in the late 1600s. If you had asked me if this were possible, I would have been very skeptical, but Lisbeth has managed to pull it off.

Her story takes what has always been dry and frankly skimpy history, at least in the mainstream history textbooks, and creates empathy through detailed layers of her characters' thoughts and emotions. Until I read it, I had no idea that such close relationships and harmony existed between the Natives and the European immigrants–that towns had even been created based on the intent to foster harmony and peaceful, diverse community. I find that a source of great hope and encouragement, still deeply relevant to current culture and the history we are creating daily now.

Sadly, also like today, not everyone at that time was interested in cultivating peace and harmony between all peoples. Then, as now, corruption also flourished, and some people hungered more for money, land, and power than for peace. Deep prejudices, racial hatred, and hideous oppression led to unthinkable acts of cruelty, murder, and war. The best and the worst in humanity showed itself on all sides of the conflicts.

I highly encourage anyone to read Lisbeth's book. You will learn more than you ever absorbed in history class. It will be more accessible, easier to identify with the participants from all sides, and more memorable—and affecting—than you can imagine. It will change you.

Lori Brown Patrick, Editor

———⚮———

I was so excited after reading Lori's words about the first half of Praying Town, that I almost forgot to tell her about Damaris's journal. Sadly, it was not found in a dusty old box shoved under the table for a hundred years in an antique store. It was not passed down from generation to generation and discovered. Damaris's journal was written by me in order to bring Damaris to life. She seemed to want to tell her story herself and so I let her do that in her journal.

When I first started to research my family tree, I came across a second-generation Plymouth Plantation couple, Jacob and Damaris Cooke, living in a place that had a reference to it as a Praying Town. Curiosity got the best of me and I just had to find out why Namasket/Middleborough were referred to as such.

It truly bothered me that I had never heard of a Praying Town before, at least not anything to the degree I began to find out about. That is when I dug deep into the scholarly research books and histories. The more I read, the more intrigued I became with this place the way it had been before the King Philip War. It was simple, almost commune-like, in the way the Christian Natives and Colonials were described as living. Then I read where King Philip's sister, Amie, was a resident there also, and the thought came to my mind that the two women knew each other. Since they must have known each other, what was their life like back in the 1600s?

Even though the history actually happened, I have had to take writer's liberty with the people who lived through it. There is no way of knowing for sure who actually knew whom and how they felt about each other. If the friendships are believable, I have succeeded in my goal of bringing these people's stories to life.

There are shocking, startling, unbelievable moments in the story. Surprisingly, those are all from actual eyewitness accounts. My fiction fills in the day-to-day moments that have been lost to time.

L. Gawenase Johnson, Author

❦Acknowledgments❦

Thank you to:

My loving husband, Roger Johnson, a.k.a. Ironbear, for his encouragement. He helped me choose a new laptop, gave me a helpful writer's guide, made it possible for me to find quiet time and places to work, and he created the leather bag used in the book's cover photograph. He also was available and willing to be my human spell-checker.

My son, Jeremiah Johnson, who encouraged me by sharing a quote: "I don't know the key to success, but the key to failure is trying to please everybody."

My daughter, Kristen Ellinger, for her help with the cover photography.

My sister Louise Sherman, who made time for me to run by her my newly written passages.

My sister Linda Dickinson for sharing the trip to Plimouth Plantation.

My friend Nancy Howorth for the initial edit. I love to listen to her read out loud.

My niece Rayna Phipps and friends Marie Bell and Jean Oien for listening.

A special thanks goes to my first-draft readers: your input challenged me to take the extra step and turn this saga into an actual novel.

Linda Dreher
Debra Kite
Louise Sherman
Monika Denasha

My biggest thanks goes to Deleyna Marr, author of *Sisterhood* and *Dominion of Darkness*, who worked one-on-one with me for hours on end to guide and direct me as to how to create a new and improved manuscript. Without her skillful tutoring, I would not have completed *Praying Town*.

Thank you to Lori Brown Patrick, my fabulous editor, for the encouragement right when I needed it most. Any errors in this book are my own.

People and Places

Tribal Names:
Algonquin tribes: People of the Dawnland (where the sun rises. Now New England)

- Abenaki
- Massachusetts
- Mohegan, also known as Mohican
- Narragansett
- Nipmuck
- Pennacooks
- Pequot
- Wabanaki
- Wampanoag

Other Tribes: People of the Longhouse, other tribes, and River villages living in what was considered the inland frontier (now New York State and New Jersey)

- Hoosacs
- Lenni-Lenapes
- Mahicansacs
- Mohawk
- Onondaga

Places:

- Assawompsett Pond
- Namasket
- Middleborough
- Plymouth Colony
- Massachusetts Bay Colony

Native People's Names:

- **Amie** (Ah-mee): daughter of Massasoit, sister of King Philip (Metcomet), wife of Tispiquin
- **Asowetow,** (Ah-so-wet-oh): daughter of Tispiquin and Amie, *aka* Betty
- **Betty**: daughter of Tispiquin and Amie, *aka* Asowetow
- **Hobomoko,** (Hoh-boh-moh-koh): early Native in Plymouth who assisted Miles Standish
- **John Sassamon** (Sass ah mon) of the Massachusetts tribe: Harvard-educated preacher and Bible translator
- **King Philip**: leader of the Wampanoag
- **Mattashunannamo, Tobias, and Wampapaquan**: King Philip's closest counselors
- **Massasoit** (Mass-ah-soit): the former supreme leader of the Wampanoag and the father of Metcomet, *aka* King Philip, and Amie
- **Maskippaque,** (Mask-skip-pa kwe): lives in Namasket praying town; served on the Sassamon trial jury
- **Mattashunannamo** (Mat-ah-shoon-ah-mo): one of King Philip's advisors
- **Meetamoo** (Meet-moo): a Wampanoag woman
- **Metcomet** (Met-com-it): second son of Massasoit, also known as King Philip; supreme leader of the Wampanoag tribe
- **Naughton** (Naw-ton): Anthony and William; Natives, they were among John Eliot's earliest converts. They became Christian missionaries
- **Ninigit** (Nin-ni-jit): King Philip's son and student of John Sassamon
- **Patuckson** (Paw-tuck-sun): an eyewitness who testified at the Sassamon trial

- **Tispiquin** (Tis-pi-qwin): the sachem (sub-chief) of Namasket, under King Philip and Plymouth; Amie's husband
- **Wootonekanuske** (Who-ton-ka-noo-ske): King Philip's wife

Wampanoag (Wah-pah-no wog) who live in the Namasket praying town:
- **Tispiquin and his wife Amie**
- **Asowetow,** *aka* Betty
- **Wampapaquan** (Wham-pa-pa-kwan): Tobias's son and part of King Philip's inner circle
- **Wampye** (Wam-pie): Wampanoag Native, childhood friend of Amie; served on Sassamon jury
- **Wannoo** (Wah-noo): Sage Elder in the praying town of Namasket; served on the Sassamon jury
- **Joseph and Mary Sipit with granddaughter Sara.** Early converts who live in praying town Namasket

Colonials living in Namasket / Middleborough praying town:

- Jacob and Damaris Cooke, son Francis, and daughter Ruth
- Ephraim Tinkham and family, wife, and mother (a woodworker and survey apprentice)
- Jabez Howland, Constable

Colonials of Plymouth:

- John and Mary Rickard, Jacob and Damaris's daughter and son-in law
- Governor Josiah Winslow

Colonials of the Massachusetts Bay Colony:

- Thomas and Sara Bond, owners of the inn
- Governor Leverett

Schaghticoke

Leffingwell
Eddy

Norwich

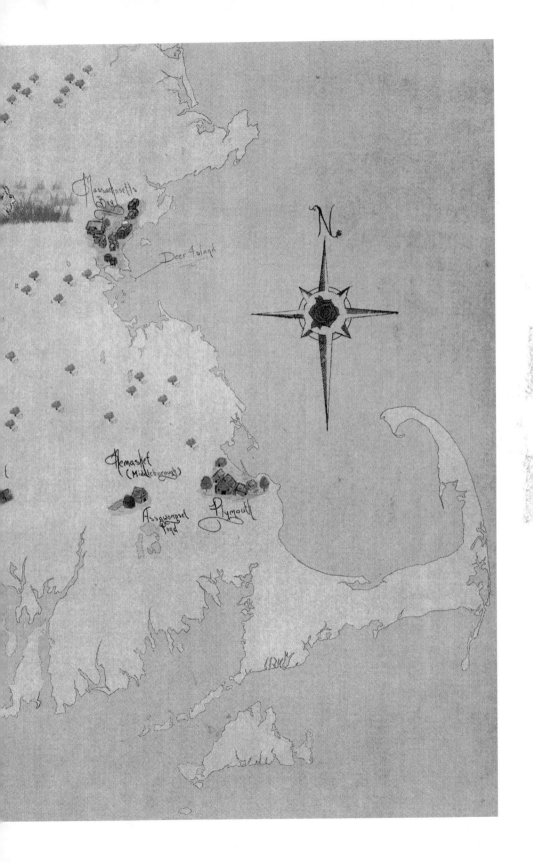

Chapter One

✤The Preacher Came A-Courting✤

Damaris

Just when the flavors of Damaris's Indian porridge were on the verge of blending, the fire began to burn down. She took a piece of wood from the wood box and placed it under the pot. She had seen that it was green, not quite ready, and now, because of her untimely use of it, the fire was too smoky for her liking. She gave her porridge a good stir, hung the soup paddle on the hook by the hearth, and crossed the room to open the cabin door.

She stepped outside. The sky was clear, with the exception of a few pink clouds standing in contrast against the blue of the expanse. Like wispy tails, they moved at a leisurely pace high above. Damaris sensed a chill in the air, yet the evening sun compelled her to close her eyes and lift her face in its direction. The sun's rays penetrated like a flight of arrows fired from the bows of the tiny forest people, the ones Amie used to tell about.

A disturbance in the bushes across the way drew her attention. Someone was nearing the opening at the end of the well-worn path that led from the Council house.

There was purpose in John Sassamon's stride as he emerged into the section of town where the cluster of hewn dwellings surrounded the cow commons. Namasket's visiting minister had been spending much of his time assisting the missionary John Eliot in the translation of the Holy Bible.

He was dressed in English attire and his hair was freshly trimmed.

Damaris stood motionless as Sassamon approached the humble abode across the earthen road and stepped onto Amie's porch. This was not the time to call out a greeting. She looked down at her doeskin skirt and linsey-woolsey top and smiled. She thought to herself, "Maybe if he lives with us long enough, he will learn to make do without the expense of imported English clothes."

Her thoughts turned to the time she and Amie first heard his deep, reverberating voice. "I wonder if he will ever know the profound influence he and John Eliot have had on all of us around here?" Damaris looked again toward Amie's door before she turned to her husband, Jacob, saying as she stepped back over the threshold to reenter the cabin, "Maybe there will be a wedding happening soon."

Jacob had planted himself in the rocking chair that the newcomer Ephraim Tinkham had brought over earlier in the day. "I like this chair." He ran his hand over the arm-rest. "The young man Tinkham and his family are moving up from Plymouth to establish themselves in the town of Middleborough. They will be good friends."

Damaris came up from behind and playfully tugged at the long cluster of hair gathered by a ribbon at the back of Jacob's neck. "What did young Mr. Tinkham want from you in exchange for that fine chair?"

"He wants me to apprentice him to survey," Jacob answered.

Damaris wanted Jacob to get up and come over to the door and take a look towards Amie's.

"Mind your business, woman," Jacob said, looking at his wife with a twinkle. "I'm not so sure that old Tispiquin's pride can handle having his daughter married to a preacher. It is hard enough on the old sachem that his wife and children attend the church meetings."

Jacob became more serious. "Damaris, Tispiquin is from Africa. He has lived a different life than we can ever imagine. He spent more than a year or two before the mast on the whaling ships, seeing the world, before he won Massasoit's favor and married your friend Amie."

Damaris glanced at her husband. "He has settled down since. He has a family and is the sachem of Namasket." Then she looked again toward Amie's. "I think that Asowetow is ready to say yes to the minister, if today he were to ask her." She stood in the doorway to watch her friend welcome the preacher into her cabin. Once he had entered and the neighbor's door was shut, she turned her attention back to Jacob. "I think Tispiquin would change his mind if only he would attend a meeting and hear John Sassamon preach God's Word. He should come to church when John speaks scripture in Algonquin."

Jacob placed his hands on the arms of the chair. "You are right about John's preaching being powerful, but have you taken into consideration that Sassamon is almost old enough to be the girl's father?" He rose from the new rocker, walked over to the hearth, backed up to it, and placed his hands behind his back. "Then again, so is Tispiquin old enough to be Amie's father, rather than her husband." He chuckled. "Perhaps that might factor into his thoughts in regard to the marriage."

Jacob paused for a moment; his countenance became serious. "Tispiquin is showing signs lately of becoming more and more caught up in the old superstitious ways. He is spending too much time listening to Amie's brother, Metcomet. If Tispiquin didn't have possession of so much land around here, well, sometimes I think he would endeavor to move his entire family over to Metcomet's camp."

"Amie would not want to leave our town. She has told me time and time again that she is through with the nomadic lifestyle," Damaris stated.

Jacob walked over to join her at the door, and together they watched John Sassamon and young Asowetow leave Amie's cabin.

Damaris smiled when she saw Asowetow's strung-corn necklace, the outward declaration of availability, peeking through her braids, and winked at Jacob when he reached out to her. "Neither would Asowetow, especially since she is going to say yes." She took hold of his hand. "He is going to ask her. I just know it." She gave his hand a squeeze. "Look at him. He is like a sturdy tree, and I can't help thinking of how wonderful it would be if he were to set down roots here in Namasket instead of one of the other praying towns."

Jacob drew Damaris into an embrace. They watched two silhouettes against the blue-pink sky on a stroll toward Assawompsett pond. "Our people need roots."

Chapter Two

✦Amie's Request✦

Damaris

The following week, Jacob, Francis, and Ephraim left to survey the new road upriver. Damaris finally had her chance to check out Jacob's new rocking chair. She ran her fingers over the smooth finish. Young Ephraim would have no trouble as Jacob's apprentice if he brought this same level of attention to surveying.

The beautifully crafted chair had a formed two-inch seat and an artful curve to the armrests. Its hand-turned spindles were defined to fit the curve of the back. Damaris's favorite feature was the beautifully painted panels spaced between the spindles. "Very lovely," she said aloud. She traced the stylized flowers and fruits with her finger.

Damaris sat comfortably in the chair and made it move forward and back while she thought about the Tinkhams and all the other newcomers that were arriving. New people would mean new roads. There would be enough survey work in the future for both her son Francis and Ephraim Tinkham.

An unexpected wave of dread came over her. Many of the new immigrants would not be like the Tinkhams. Newcomers were often self-serving and greedy. They wouldn't all have a heart for the local natives the same way as those who were settling in the praying towns. Some newcomers tended to be only interested in the acquisition of Indian land and didn't seem to want to take into consideration the harm they caused to those who wanted to live in harmony with the land.

Later in the day she put a fresh kettle of corn soup to simmer over a bed of slow coals, and called her daughter, Ruth, to join her in a visit to Amie's.

Ruth was eager to go outside, where she loved to be. "Wipe that dirt off your face before we leave," Damaris reminded her. She considered calling the girl back to redo her braids but accepted things as they were, remembering that Amie and Asowetow were accustomed to the habits of her nine-year-old.

As they crossed the road, Damaris felt a chill in the air. She glanced back at her house, so warm and cozy. She tapped Ruth on the shoulder and pointed toward the casement. "There is a tear in the oil paper. Don't let me forget to tell your father that it will need to be replaced before the cold weather comes."

Hard to believe that only two days before, the unseasonably warm weather had been perfect for the town's harvest feast. The annual affair happened after all the hard labor to bring in the corn and flax. They enjoyed meeting to sing joyous chants and psalms of thanksgiving. John Sassamon preached in Algonquin, and if that wasn't enough to be thankful for, Tispiquin stood up with his wife Amie to announce the betrothal of their daughter Asowetow to John Sassamon, with the wedding set to take place in a few weeks.

The Bible that John Sassamon read from was the culmination of John Eliot's passion to bring the gospel of Jesus Christ to Native people in their own tongue. John's ministry had proven successful with a great many other villages. The Nipmuck praying town, where he began the ministry, was his largest community of believers.

If Metcomet's band of Wampanoag were to settle in one place, they would form a massive settlement and become the largest town around, even bigger than Nipmuck. Damaris believed that Amie would be delighted if her brother's band formed a praying town, and she knew that she and Jacob would.

Damaris loved visiting with Amie when the men were away. The inside of Amie's house was decorated with simple woven mats and soft fur rugs. There were utilitarian embroidered bags and attractive baskets hanging on the walls from wooden pegs. These were used for storage in the same way that Damaris used the wooden boxes her father and mother brought over from England.

Amie brought an earthenware cup filled with black birch tea and handed it to Damaris where she sat on a comfortable rug. "You want some, too?" Amie inquired of Ruth, already going to the hearth to pour the girl a cup. She handed it to Ruth and turned back to Damaris. "John Sassamon has been to my brother's camp recently."

Amie sat close and stared into her cup for a moment. Damaris waited, curious what news Amie had.

Her friend glanced up and met her eyes. "Have you heard that Metcomet has taken on the English name of Philip?"

Damaris shook her head and Amie continued. "When Sassamon returned, he told us that Metcomet has decided to use his English name when interacting with the settlements. I overheard John tell Tispiquin that my brother asked him what English title indicated a supreme leader. John told him that the colonies answer to the King of England."

Amie brought her hand across her chest. "My brother told John Sassamon that he was in the position of king over all the sachems of the Wampanoag. He wants to be addressed as King Philip." She brought her hand down and took a sip of her tea.

Damaris smiled and raised her brow. "Well, he seems to be adopting at least some English ways. Maybe soon he will let John talk to him of our Lord."

Amie took a sip of tea and reached for the new grammar book. "In John Sassamon's absence, Asowetow and I have been filling in at the council house. We are using John Eliot's latest Algonquin grammar book," she held it up, "for teaching the locals to read and write in the native language."

Damaris reached for the book and lifted it up to her nose. She breathed in deeply from the pages. "I like the smell of a freshly printed book." After looking the book over, she handed it to Ruth. "Learning the Algonquin language has helped Jacob with his surveying. Ruth and I enjoy joining Jacob in his studies. I'm sure the Tinkhams will value the Algonquin language that is being taught."

"Many natives are learning English as well. The only thing that would make life in this commonwealth any better would be if Metcomet would settle here," Amie said.

"Everyone around Namasket knows that Sassamon has been spending a considerable amount of time traveling back and forth to meetings with your brother Metcomet at the clam beach." Damaris corrected herself, "I mean, Philip." She sipped her tea.

"King Philip." Amie shook her head and laughed. "It will be hard to get used to calling my brother by his English title. I am praying they will agree to winter with us after the corn harvest this year."

Damaris's eyes focused on Amie, searching. "It would be in their best interest to do so."

"I'm not so sure he will." Amie's brown eyes seemed distant. "John Sassamon told us that Philip has broken down the summer camp and is heading southwest to the corn fields at Mount Hope." She sipped her tea and set the cup on the floor. "As soon as their harvest is in, he plans to take his people inland for winter camp."

Amie leaned in toward Damaris. "Metcomet loves his migratory lifestyle, even if it means that the Plymouth Magistrates will expect him to turn in his armament." She picked her drink up and took a sip, then sat there gazing into the cup. "The good news is," Amie's eyes rose with a hint of hope, "John Sassamon was quite excited to report that he helped my brother to write to Plymouth about this."

Damaris leaned in toward Amie with the warm earthenware cup cradled in her hands. "But that was the reason Metcomet, I mean Philip, invited John Sassamon to come over to the shore, wasn't it? He wanted to learn to read and write."

Amie brought more tea and settled back down near Damaris. "My brother is stubborn and set in his ways. He doesn't see things the same as we do," she sighed. "However, he has agreed to allow his son, Ninigit, to stay for a time with John Sassamon in order for him to learn to read and write. Perhaps at least he will be allowed to winter here."

Damaris and Amie each had a few treasures passed down to them by their parents. Damaris noticed that Ruth was looking at the red English riding coat displayed on Amie's wall. "Ruth, your grandfather Stephen Hopkins and Governor Winslow gave that coat to Amie's father, Massasoit, when they first met. It happened long before Amie and I were born."

Ruth reached up to touch the fifty-year-old token of friendship.

Amie said, "My father, Massasoit, gave the coat to Tispiquin, who still wears it on special occasions. You may possibly see him wear it at Asowetow's wedding."

Damaris's reaction mirrored Amie's joy. "It is so exciting! We're going to have a wedding! I am willing to help you in any way I can. Asowetow couldn't have found a better husband."

"Tomorrow is John Sassamon's land walk." Amie set her cup down. "I want you to witness it. I'll come for you in the morning."

Damaris nodded but was distracted by a rumble from the back of Amie's home.

Amie sighed. "It's Tispiquin. He must be back from his visit to the shore." The commanding presence of Amie's husband filled the room.

Tispiquin was dressed in leather leggings and a breechclout. His black, crinkly hair was well greased and flattened down against his head by a leather headband surmounted with woven wampum. He carried two wampum belts crossed over his well-oiled upper body. This impressive show of wealth covered much of his tattooed chest. He was girded with a woven sash that held a belt bag and a porcupine quill–embroidered sheath. The sheath held a knife that was more than just for show.

His voice reverberated within the small room. "I have been taking apart bark wigwams for Metcomet. He is on the move to harvest the corn fields." Tispiquin pulled the ball-headed pagamigon from his belt and hung the war club on a hook before he turned toward Damaris and Ruth. "I seen

Jacob take the new Middleborough fellow upriver with him and Francis this morning."

"I expect they will be back before nightfall." Damaris set down her cup and stood, preparing to leave. "You should see the beautiful chair the young Mr. Tinkham made for a trade."

Tispiquin lowered himself to the floor. "I never liked chairs much." He adjusted the fur rug and grinned. Damaris and Ruth picked up the pottery cups and handed them to Amie. "You won't want to miss the land walk tomorrow."

"We won't," Damaris said, waving goodbye to Amie and placing her arm around Ruth. "Tomorrow's event will be something for you to witness," she told her daughter. When they arrived at the cabin door, she let go of Ruth and lifted the wooden latch. "Tomorrow you will be there to see how much land John Sassamon will be able to claim to build a home for his bride." She smiled, "It will be your first time."

ASOWETOW

Lisbeth Guwanuse Johnson

Chapter Three

✿The Land Walk✿

Amie

The next morning Amie arrived at Damaris's door just as she had promised. "Hasten, you don't want to miss John's land walk." Amie looked beyond Damaris, who had just opened the door, and said to Jacob, "Tispiquin has agreed to allow John and Asowetow to obtain for themselves a tract of land by using the old tradition." There was no keeping the excitement out of her voice. Her attention turned back to Damaris. "Assawompsett Pond is her favorite place, so he has chosen to make his walk close to the pond."

Amie led Damaris, her family, and the townspeople on the walk toward the pond. Many who followed her were the Wampanoag she had grown up with, like Wannoo, Wampye, Maskippaque, and the Sipit families. They were joined by her new Christian brothers and sisters like Ephraim and Mary Tinkham.

The women carried baskets and woven bags. Amie kept the lead on the path southwest from the cow commons. The curious bovines joined the procession until their primitive fencing barred their way. She glanced back to see the cows watching the humans continue on down the path. She felt their yearning to participate.

The entourage came to the clearing where Tispiquin was giving John Sassamon and Asowetow counsel. Amie smiled lovingly at her husband in his role of Namasket's Black Sachem. The newcomers were greeted by the pungent incense of a small ceremonial fire where a braid of sweet-grass was still smoldering. Sweet aesthesis accompanied the prayers of the young couple up to the Creator of all things. Amie stepped up behind the couple and placed her hands on their shoulders. "God in heaven, Creator of all the world and giver of life, bless my daughter and son to be with joy and prosperity." The hoot of an owl from the depths of the woods and a high-pitched call from a red-tailed hawk punctuated her prayer. Amie stepped back to her place.

Amie noticed her daughter gaze up toward John Sassamon and saw his face respond to Asowetow's admiration. Then she watched him take hold of her hand. When he spoke, Amie noticed that her daughter was giving all her attention to John Sassamon and wondered if she was listening to the words of her father. Tispiquin explained, "A man is expected to be a good hunter to provide meat for his family. I will expect that from you."

John listened to his future father-in-law's sage advice. When Tispiquin finished, the young minister turned to address his flock.

"At a time like this we should bring our hearts and minds together in prayer to our Lord Jesus Christ for His blessing upon us. The walk I'm about to embark on represents more than just my marriage to the beautiful Asowetow." Then he turned and looked intently at each person. Amie felt the sincerity of John's love for the Christian believers. "I will be making a commitment to becoming your full-time pastor. I need your approval before I accept the land here."

"A-ho A-ho. We approve," the townspeople said in unison.

Amie turned to Damaris and shared a satisfied smile. They would have a full-time minister, and her daughter would have a wonderful husband.

John Sassamon removed his woolen jacket and gave it to Asowetow for safekeeping. The lovers' eyes met for a moment before Tispiquin addressed Sassamon, giving him a review of the custom. "You seek out a rock." His chest became large when he threw back his shoulders. Amie felt her own heart swell with pride. She had a wonderful husband. "Make sure you find one that will be big enough for Jacob to see it when he surveys." He continued to hold the strong pose as he gave Jacob a quick glance with a slight smile. The crowd chuckled. "You are permitted to place the boulder by a tree of your choice." They chuckled again at his use of the word boulder. Sassamon was not laughing. Amie guessed that for John Sassamon, this whole ordeal was a most pleasant torture. Next to Tispiquin, the minister looked small and weak, and yet there was determination in the way he stretched and flexed his muscles.

Amie's thoughts were interrupted by the commanding voice of her husband. "Find another rock and place it by another tree as you go. This will mark the territory I will give for you and Asowetow to make your home, being as she is as intent as her mother on staying in one place."

Amie smiled at Tispiquin's words and watched with anticipation when he crossed his arms and took a few steps to the east, then turned to the west before he stood in front of Sassamon. He glanced at her and nodded before he continued to address the crowd. "Because I wish to please my wife and daughter," he turned his attention back to Sassamon, "I will not hold you to a walk, you will be free to run as fast and far as you can and meet us all here before the sun is overhead."

Could it be that Tispiquin had softened his heart towards this marriage? His face hardened in an effort to look stern. "If you are too tenderfoot to endure the challenge, then the wedding is off."

Amie sighed and the assemblage murmured. John Sassamon nodded to the Sachem. No doubt John understood that the battle today was not only for the land, but for the Black Sachem's approval. This Sassamon was a good man, good for her daughter and good for the town. He would prove himself worthy today, she hoped. The sun reflected from the silver ball and cone dangling from Sassamon's ear when he moved to speak to her and the others. Amie felt reverent when John took one step back, crossed his arms, bowed his head and closed his eyes.

After what seemed like a long time, he raised his head, uncrossed his arms, took a deep breath, and turned his attention to his parishioners. "Please excuse my lack of modesty. My intent is wholesome." He removed his shirt, exposing his lightly tanned naked torso.

Amie giggled to see the sharp contrast that his upper body made in comparison to his tanned face. John handed the linen garment to Asowetow, her daughter, whose eyes fluttered up, then quickly down toward the wild aster flowers and milkweed near her feet.

Everyone's attention turned to Tispiquin when he drew the ball-headed war club from his girded waist and raised it high in the air. "When I bring this down it will be the signal for you to go." Only a short moment lapsed before his pagamigon came down and his voice boomed, "Yat-tah-hey! Yat-tah-hey!" The crowd yelled, "Yat-tah-hey Yat-tah-hey!" and made a ruckus. John struck out from the meadow, down the path and out of sight.

This event would take a while, so the men sat down in the grass.

There were milkweeds ready for the harvest in the meadow. Amie had been holding tight to her gathering bag. "Let us go see how much milkweed down we can gather while John is on his run," she said. The women set out to gather the useful, soft down.

Tispiquin

Tispiquin joined Wannoo, Jacob, and the other men who were seated in the grass. Grasshoppers were all about, hopping some good lengths from one milkweed to another. There was silence. The men watched the women in the distance and the propulsion of grasshoppers. Wannoo pulled his small knife from the neck sheath that hung in front of his linsey-woolsey shirt. He picked up a stick and began to whittle. "It is nice to have an excuse to take a rest."

Tispiquin looked over to see that the women were on the far side of the meadow before he reached into his pouch. He drew out a small, salt-glazed ceramic flask that held his medicinal firewater. He took a sip, made a face, shook his head, and said, "Ahhh, I think Sassamon will do well in Namasket." His eyes scanned the faces of those present. "He gets on well with you pray-to-Jesus people." He took another sip, then passed the flask to Jacob, giving him an assuring nod, "And you pray-to-Jesus colonials." He dropped and raised his head. "As long as you pay my due as your Sachem, you can pray and live however you want." He watched Jacob take a sip and pass the rum to Wannoo.

"You have it pretty good, old man," Tispiquin said to Wannoo. "I see that these days you get to sit around instead of hunting." Then Tispiquin gave Wannoo a friendly poke and bellowed, "Mighty hunter goes to the pen of the big-eyed-pig. Pig looks up to mighty Wannoo with his wide eyes, saying, 'Wannoo, take me.'"

The men laughed.

Maskippaque took the flask from Wannoo and held it up to his lips in a gesture of respectful participation, with abstinence. "I got a bear on my last hunt upriver before your Philip sold the hunting grounds. That big boy was not in a pen." Then he passed the rum to Wampye and nodded toward Jacob and the others. "We should go on a hunt before the wedding to provide for the kettle."

Wampye made the respectful gesture of abstinence before the eager hand of Francis took hold.

"I agree," he said. Jacob's lad held the flask in his right hand and lifted it into the air. "To the hunt," he said with display, and proceeded to nearly choke on the rum. His face turned red. He coughed and carried on.

The men laughed out loud at the effect the hot liquid had on the youth.

Young Tinkham took the flask from Francis and mimicked Maskippaque and Wampye before he passed it back to Tispiquin. "Another detail to tend to. I hear that the wood for Asowetow's cabin is hewn and stacked. I'm willing to help."

"We have everything set ready to go," said Wannoo. "It won't take long to build if we work together. I will supervise."

Tispiquin looked yonder, not wanting the womenfolk to see the flask, and quickly slipped his salt-glazed container into his over-the-shoulder bag. He pulled out dried venison and passed the meat around to the men just as the women returned with their arms full.

Tispiquin looked upward to evaluate where the sun was.

"He should be coming out of the woods soon," Asowetow said, and looked expectantly towards the path. She was still holding tight to John's shirt and coat.

Tispiquin smiled innocently at his wife. The women, and even little Ruth, came with woven bags filled with milkweed fluff. His wife was good. They would have a warm, soft bed this winter. He reached into his bag for more of his venison to share with the women.

Mary Sipit and Mary Tinkham had gone to the wild black-cap berries and filled two baskets to add to the dried meat, making a good snack to share as they waited.

They ate and waited quietly until the group heard autumn leaves crackle to the rhythm of the runner's feet. The entire assemblage rose. Jacob helped Wannoo up, and Tispiquin turned to greet the man who would marry his daughter.

Amie

Amie pointed in the direction of the sound. "Here he comes," she said. John's sweat-drenched body came up the path. Damaris nudged her and said softly, "With that much perspiration, it looks like he may have made a better run than many a younger man."

Then the others also saw the shirtless figure emerge from the woods.

"Yat-tah-hey! Well done! Yat-tah-hey!" was the out-burst of heartfelt cheers from the assemblage when John ran by. Tispiquin drew a soft doeskin from his bandoleer bag and handed it to John Sassamon so that he could wipe his brow.

Amie joyously watched her husband become absorbed in the excitement. He stared intently at the exhausted young man. Tispiquin placed his hand on John's shoulder. Amie felt a gentle tension leave her neck. She turned to Damaris and spoke into her ear. "I think today, John Sassamon has won Tispiquin's full approval." Then she turned her atten-tion toward where the foundation for the minister's house had already been laid. "The town started the minister's home close to the Council house. Asowetow told me that she likes the location of their cabin."

She looked back towards the commons. She wouldn't be able to see Asowetow's house from her own. Amie sighed, "I wish my house faced toward them."

"Mine does," Damaris assured her.

"I want to keep an eye on my daughter when her hus-band is traveling."

Tispiquin turned to Jacob. "You can do the survey now."

Jacob, Francis, and Ephraim Tinkham picked up their accouterments and headed down the path toward Assa-wompsett Pond.

On their way back home, Amie and Damaris lagged behind the crowd. Damaris was quite caught up in the excite-ment. "Would you like for me to go with you to Plymouth to settle the title?" she asked.

"Oh Damaris, thank you for offering." Amie took her hand in appreciation. "The land will be in Asowetow's name. Tispiquin and I wish it so."

Damaris made no comment regarding the decision. "We will stay with my daughter Mary. She lives in Plymouth. I have had the desire to visit her and would not consider you making the journey alone."

Amie knew how much Damaris missed her daughter, Mary Rickard. Her friend would be able to see her granddaughter, little Mary, as well. It would be a good trip for them both.

"I expect she will willingly welcome us," Damaris continued.

Tispiquin

The next day, Tispiquin and the other men gathered at the council house. They sat around on benches moved in close to form a casual circle to hear the news. John Sassamon sat on the bench next to Wannoo and waited for the crew to give a report of the survey. He still looked tired. Once Ephraim had arrived, Jacob made the announcement. "We plumbed every rock and tree and the total of John Sassamon's run measured out to be three hundred and fifty-five acres."

Tispiquin smiled. A good run. He nodded at his future son-in-law.

"Yat-tah-hey. Three hundred and fifty-five acres," the gathered men repeated.

"Well done, John Sassamon. Well done." Wannoo patted John's back. He looked directly over at the Black Sachem with a twinkle in his eye and said for all to hear, "Now Tispiquin will not be able to trade good hunting ground off to strangers."

The sudden comment was a blow. Tispiquin kept his expression unreadable as the other men laughed at what was more than just a harmless jest.

Chapter Four

❧Plymouth❧

Excerpt from the writings of Damaris Cooke,
1677 Massachusetts.

I don't know if it was because he was about to
marry Asowetow and was thinking about true love,
or if he thought I needed to be reminded of what
God had to say about love, but we received a sermon
about love. It was before Amie and I headed out to
Plymouth. I remember John Sassamon's words as he
read the Bible. They were like music. His voice was
smooth and beautiful like the leaf of a lamb's ear
in springtime. He read a verse that has never left
my mind. Jesus had spoken to his disciples: "This is
my commandment, that ye love one another, as I
have loved you." To this day it continues to play in
my mind when I think about my friendship with
Amie. The other verse that repeated was, "Greater
love hath no man than this, that a man lay down
his life for his friends." John 15:13

Damaris

Damaris sat with a small assemblage of women and children on the bench along the west side of the lodge the town used for meetings. She was facing the men who sat across the room on the east side. John Sassamon stood at the north end, near the fireplace. There was also a fireplace at the south end, driving the autumn chill from the air. Only the very young sons stayed close to their mothers. Tispiquin was away assisting King Philip.

Damaris fell into the deep, hypnotic beauty of John's voice when he read 1 Corinthians 13 from the Algonquin translation. His voice nearly lulled her to sleep. She listened to its rhythmic cadence, like listening to a song. She did not focus on its meaning as much as its beauty, but when he read aloud in English it caused her to sit up and pay attention. "Today I am going to talk to you about love. Charity is another word for love. When the Bible speaks of charity, I want you to think of the love you have in your heart for others." She glanced at Jacob and Francis, took hold of Ruth's hand, and focused her attention on the preacher. "Charity suffereth long, and is kind; charity envieth not; charity vaunteth not itself, is not puffed up, doth not behave itself unseemly, seeketh not her own, is not easily provoked, thinketh no evil, rejoiceth not in iniquity, but rejoiceth in the truth; beareth all things, believeth all things, hopeth all things, endureth all things. Charity never faileth, but whether *there be* prophecies, they shall fail; whether there be tongues, they shall cease; whether *there be* knowledge, it shall vanish away. For we know in part, and we prophesy in part. But when that which is perfect is come, then that which is in part shall be done away."

After John read from the scriptures, Damaris paid attention to the sermon about love. One of the highlights that impressed her was when John Sassamon spoke about *agape* love. She heard the truth about love, and just as she was beginning to feel she was unable to live up to God's expectation, John Sassamon's voice rose in conclusion. "And now abideth faith, hope, charity, these three; but the greatest of these is charity."

———٭———

The night before the trek to Plymouth, Damaris stood by the side of her bed in her small cabin and laid out some hard bread and jerked meat, a baby blanket for her granddaughter, and a change of clothes to pack into her shoulder bag. When she tested it for weight, she removed the change of clothes and blanket. She wondered if Amie was bringing a change of clothes. The Bible verse came back into her head again. "Greater love hath no man than this, that a man lay down his life for his friends."

If someone tried to rob them, would she be able to lay down her life for Amie? She re-folded the little woolen baby blanket she had made on her tiny nineteen-inch loom and placed it back into her bag.

———٭———

After an uneventful trek from Namasket, the first place Damaris wanted to see in Plymouth was her oldest daughter Mary Rickard's house. When Mary and John Rickard first married, she and Jacob had tried to get the new Rickards to move up to Namasket to become a part of the excitement of the new Christian community that was proving that Natives and colonials could live together for the glory of God. Instead, her daughter and son-in-law chose to build their home in Plymouth and raise their children in a place that was becoming overrun with the kind of people Damaris thought of as wharf rats.

The last time Damaris and Jacob had visited, Mary's husband had barely started the foundation on the land where

Damaris's father's inn had been. The last Damaris knew, they were still living in the basement and had not started to build the actual house.

When they arrived, Damaris was amazed that John had completed a beautiful, symmetrical house. Amie pointed her finger, drawing Damaris's attention to its high, triangular roof. "It is so high up."

Damaris pointed out the leaded glass windows with their closeable wooden shutters hinged and opened to the right side of each opening. "There is glass in the windows up there, can you see? That is not oil paper." Then she pointed to a solid, massive chimney that stood on the south end. "That fireplace would dwarf any of the hearths we have back in Namasket." She paused, looked down, and confessed, "I had so hoped that Mary would have been content to live like us, and put her focus on serving the Lord and not on possessing material things."

"I don't know," said Amie, "I've only been inside a house like this once. It belonged to Captain Standish. My father brought me with him when he went to visit Hobomoko when he lived with the Captain. It wasn't as big of a house as this one, but it was bigger than any single dwelling I had ever been in. They let me explore inside." Amie's face lit up a bit. "Someday, I might like to live in a bigger house." She smiled at Damaris. "You look at me so funny. You know I am most satisfied with my own home."

Damaris smiled at her friend. "The biggest home I was ever able to explore was in Massachusetts Bay Colony. My father had a friendship with the Bonds, owners of an inn up there. They had a son, Thomas, my age, and when my father and I made a trip, Thomas showed me all around." Damaris looked at Amie and said, "I would like for us to go visit them someday. I want to take Ruth there to meet the Bonds. My father told me that we are somehow related."

Damaris stepped up to the heavy wooden door and knocked. Amie was by her side when the door opened. Mary's face lit up when she saw her mother. There was instantaneous joy as Damaris and Mary stepped back to get a better look at each other.

"Mother, how long are you here for?"

"As soon as the office opens tomorrow, Amie is registering the marriage of Asowetow and John Sassamon, along with their land deed. John is our new minister." Damaris's voice revealed her excitement when she smiled at Amie and then Mary. "You remember Asowetow? She is so grown up now, you might not recognize her." Mary's features bore a smudge mark. It looked to Damaris as if Mary might have run her soiled hand across her cheek, not missing her nose. Quickly Mary drew up the corner of her apron to wipe her face, leaving the telltale signs of ashes on the white cloth. Damaris suspected they had taken her away from a household chore.

"We need a place to stay the night. Amie is registering the land, then we need to go back to Namasket in a timely manner, but Amie and I have time, and can give you a hand with whatever you are doing," Damaris offered.

Mary's head dropped down and then she looked up at Amie with a half smile. "My dear," she said in an overly sweet voice, "congratulations to your daughter. I hope you don't mind waiting out here for a moment. I have something that I need to discuss privately with my mother."

Mary escorted her mother into the parlor and shut the door, leaving Amie to wait on the porch. "I don't want that Wampanoag women staying in my house overnight," she said.

Damaris stepped back, her mouth dropped open. The blood drained from her face. She struggled for words to respond to her daughter's rudeness. How had her daughter come so far from the way she'd been raised? She stared at Mary's face, crushed by the disgust she saw written in her daughter's twisted lips.

After a moment, Mary's expression softened. "I suppose she could sleep in the livery."

"I don't think so." The circulation began to return to Damaris's face as the blood of anger rushed back to her cheeks. "If Amie is expected to sleep out there, then I will sleep in the barn with her. For that matter, Miss Mary Elizabeth Rickard, Amie and I can just go over to the inn," she said, knowing full well she and Amie didn't bring enough wampum for the inn.

Mary's lips tightened. "Mother, you don't understand. My husband has been hearing some awful things, and more than a few of the men around here don't trust her brother Philip. Did you know that he wants us to call him King Philip?" She brought her hands to her hips. "The 'King,' Tobias, and the rest of his lot come to town and strut around all decked out so proud and arrogant. Tobias was flashing a rifle and was shouting something about pigs just the other day." Mary pointed through the wall toward where Amie was waiting. "So why should we trust her? She is King Philip's sister."

"She is my best friend. That is why." Damaris stared back at her daughter in disbelief. "I sincerely hope that Amie never finds out how poorly my daughter is behaving. I don't know what I did wrong in raising you. We don't seem to see eye to eye on the natives, or religion for that matter. Are Jacob and I an embarrassment to you?"

She pointed to the old, leather-bound book sitting on the table. "Have you forgotten 'Love your neighbor as yourself'? You don't even try to understand. Just look at this place." Damaris waved her hand and pointed at all the material things about the big house. "God, sharing the gospel of Jesus, and the simple life are what is important. Someday you will get your priorities straight. I sure hope so."

"Mother." Mary motioned with her hand to keep the volume down. "The baby is asleep." Her facial expression softened. "I am truly sorry that my lifestyle upsets you." Mary's shoulders relaxed, the plumpness returned to her lips, and her eyes became normal again. "I will do my best to accommodate your friend Amie, only please don't get into an argument with my husband." Mary let out a sigh from deep within. "There is a great deal of talk among the menfolk around here and it is not favorable toward your friend's older brother. But I will do my best to keep my husband from knowing that your friend is Philip's sister."

Damaris and Amie settled into the small back room Mary provided them for the night. Sleep came easily after a full day of travel.

The next morning Damaris rose early to say goodbye to Mary and spent a coveted moment with her grandchild while her daughter fixed breakfast. After giving little Mary the blanket, Damaris took the child upon her knee. "I'm very excited that John Sassamon and Asowetow are getting married. Asowetow goes by Betty sometimes now, but I'm not used to it." Little Mary wriggled in Damaris's lap, holding her new woolen blanket. She settled as they talked.

Mary rose to stir her pot of porridge and looked over her shoulder toward her mother. "I know Betty is a nice girl, but what do you really know about the Indian man she is getting married to? I hear that he spends a lot of time over at King Philip's camp. That can't be good."

"John Sassamon is a wonderful man. If you met him you would see what I'm saying. He was raised in the Bay Colony and has had an education. He has studied at Harvard and has been assisting John Eliot with translating the Bible into Algonquin. We at Namasket are blessed to have a man of God like him in our village." Damaris shifted her grandchild to relieve the pressure. "We are in hopes that John Sassamon will be able to reach Philip and his people with the gospel of Jesus and accept our invitation to settle in Namasket permanently."

"You can trust the Indians if you want, but the men at the tavern say that Amie's brother, Philip, is amassing arms and stirring up the sachems 'round about. We have heard say that the Pequot and Narragansett were in powwow with Philip. You know that is not good, especially since they had been enemies with each other for years, and now they are meeting together." On her way back to her chair, she snatched her toddler from her mother's lap, as if protecting little Mary from some harm Damaris might impart. "Your dear friend Amie is Philip's sister. Do you really think that if we should ever have go to war with Philip that she and that savage husband of hers won't turn on you and father?"

Damaris looked down at her deerskin skirt and straightened the linsey-woolsey blouse over the empty place on her lap where the child had been. Her eyes opened wide. She sought understanding from her daughter. "John Sassamon and William Naughton have been making progress with their visits to Philip's camp. They have been making a good effort to convince Philip to settle the Wampanoag up in the Namasket area. Jacob and I believe that their joining

the praying towns and villages will be the way of the future."
She stood up. "You and John are missing out on the good
spiritual and cultural sharing that is happening in Namasket,
just like Amie's brother. We are learning from each other. It
is a simple life, and we are so blessed to have so many new
praying Indians coming to settle in Namasket. Not only that,
Namasket is not the only Christian commonwealth that is
growing. John Eliot reports of many other praying towns.
They are all thriving. Many Indians are learning to read and
write."

There came a light knock on the kitchen door. Amie
quietly made her way in and found a place next to Damaris.

Mary served the hot porridge before they took their
leave.

If Amie had sensed an undercurrent in the Rickard
household, she never let on.

It was still early when Amie and Damaris walked around the
town taking everything in. "Look," said Damaris, "they have
taken down the old Meeting House where we first heard
John Eliot preach. See, they replaced it with a new town hall."
She pointed to the newly built county seat. "That is where
you are to go and get the papers filed when they open." Then
she pointed across the street toward the new white church
that had rows of tall arched windows and a high bell tower in
the front. To the right of the door there was a sign that said
First Congregational Church of Plymouth. "A lot has changed
since we were growing up. It is hard to believe."

They passed the path on the edge of the town that led
along the heights. Amie's face lit up as she pointed to the

way into its wooded path and said, "Do you think that our trees are still there?"

"I haven't been along that path for years," Damaris answered, filled with anticipation. "We have time. Let's go and see."

"Remember when this was the best place for gathering sassafras?" Amie asked.

"It was fun to gather." Damaris found a small sassafras plant and chose from the multi-shaped leaves one shaped like a mitten, picked it, and brought it to her nose. "Wampanoag always said it helped to thin the blood after the long winter." She smiled at Amie. "I knew where to find you because they sent you here to gather when your family arrived in Plymouth after winter camp. Do you have any idea of how excited I used to get when Wampanoag would start to appear in the springtime? First there would be just one or two men in dugout canoes, and then some more would come in. And you always seemed to be with the last ones to arrive."

Amie smiled brighter. "I felt the same way. I couldn't wait to see you again." She paused in a moment of reflection. "My father was the person in charge and he wanted to ensure that everyone made it to summer camp safely, so we were always last."

For the most part, the path was the same as they remembered, except that it showed considerable wear and was wider in many places. The roots of the ancient hardwoods exposed to the foot traffic had a shiny surface. To the east they were able to look through sparse bushes and trees and see the glistening bay. The water was calm, and there was only a light breeze, just enough to keep them comfortable. To the west of the path there were many more trees, maiden ferns, lupine, and Jewell weed. Damaris reached down to touch some of the translucent Jewell weed seed pods. Pop! "Ah. Ah." She laughed at herself for jumping because the little oblong pods popped to scatter seeds.

People and animals had made tiny single-file paths that webbed here and there throughout the woods. If one should follow them they would seem to lead in circles back to where they started. Somewhere in this maze, Amie and Damaris had a secret symbol of friendship. "I hope we can find it," said Amie.

"Me too," replied Damaris. "It can't be too far from here, as I recall."

Friendship Trees

They tried to see if the old parent elm was visible from the main path, but neither of them could see it. There was too much other vegetation, especially the maple trees that were in their glory of vibrant, bright yellow, red, orange, rust, and brown. A short way down a side path they saw the tree they had been looking for. Sure enough, there were two junior elm trees growing side by side on the cusp of the gully where they had been planted. Strangely, the saplings had grown together at the trunk as if they were one tree. They noticed there was a distinct line and indentation indicating where each seedling had once been its own tree.

"I think we have planted them too close together." Amie ran her hand up the connecting line that was indented about the distance between the tip of her finger to the first joint. "I thought we had given them plenty of room back when we first planted them."

"Who knew they would have grown this much in such a short period of time?" Damaris said.

"Damaris, it has been over twenty-five years."

Damaris placed her hand on the seam of the fused trees, then turned her attention toward Amie. "I like the way they grew together like that."

Amie placed her hand back on the tree as well. "Like our friendship." They stood together in silence for a time. "I'm glad we came here."

"I am, too."

———✤———

When Amie and Damaris reentered Plymouth, they observed the many recently built houses and more that were under construction.

Damaris tried to visualize it the way it had been. "The new houses are sizable and they all use glass for their windows these days." She pointed to one nearby. "People aren't using oil paper anymore, and that reminds me that I must make sure I remind Jacob to repair ours. Maybe I should tell him that I want to replace it with glass."

There was a considerable citizenry hustling and bustling about. "Who are these people?" Amie asked. "Where do they all come from?"

Damaris felt an irresistible urge to smile in response to Amie's question. She glanced around, noting that the majority of the new faces were certainly not Indian. "I know as much as you do about the lands across the ocean, only what people who have seen them have told me. Perhaps the place is very small and they are running out of room over there." Their attention turned to the pier below. They watched a ruck of disheveled men disembark from a tall ship.

"The kinds of people that have been arriving these days are not very nice, if you ask me," Amie stated. "They remind me of the sailors who were with Tispiquin when I first met him." She blushed. "Their behavior did not please the Lord." Amie lowered and raised her eyes.

"Maybe the people who are coming down the gangplank were kicked out of England for bad behavior and sent here as a punishment." Damaris became serious. "Yesterday I overheard Jacob and Ephraim saying that the new homesteaders upriver would rather work on the Sabbath than come to worship."

"It is sad," Amie said. "There was a time when I thought that all Englishmen feared God." Amie's eyes filled with emotion when she looked toward Damaris. "I have since learned otherwise."

They approached the building where the filing was to be done. It was open and alive with people. Amie found a place in line. Damaris stayed with her friend while she waited to speak with the clerk about registering the property. Suddenly Amie's body tensed at the sound of a distinctly familiar, aggravated voice. She stood up on her toes and looked toward the sound. The crowd were focused on their own personal business, but Amie's face came to life. She looked at Damaris and said, "I recognize that voice. It's my brother."

Philip was dressed in leather leggings and a breech-clout, with a long linen shirt belted with woven wampum. The stalwart Wampanoag leader was speaking with Governor Prence, who was sitting at a heavy desk and was attended by other magistrates.

Governor Prence looked around at the other men who were standing to his left, right, and behind him before his attention came back to the Indian. "Lately we have heard many rumors gone to and fro of the rising of Indians against the English."

Amie and Damaris seemed to be the only ones within the busy hub of people who were paying attention to the silence between Phillip and the magistrates, an otherwise unnoticed silence that seemed to go on for an eternity. Amie and Damaris watched King Philip's full lips pull thin and his eyes squeeze small. He crossed his arms over his chest.

Amie's brother focused long and hard on the seated governor. "The horses, cows, and pigs have caused much damage to our corn fields. You do nothing about it. That is why my people have been making bows and arrows and fixing up guns in order to put a stop to this."

"Next," the record-keeper called.

Amie went forward to take care of her business. "I wish to put three hundred and fifty acres into my daughter's name," Amie told the registrar, and presented the survey of three hundred and fifty acres that set forth the neck of the Assawompsett pond.

"What is her English name?" asked the nervous, thin, pale little man behind the counter.

"Her English name is Betty. We call her Asowetow. Write it down as belonging to Betty Asowetow Sassamon."

The clerk dipped his quill into the ink well and wrote all the information down correctly, took the strings of wampum from Amie, and stamped the official deed to the land. "Betty's Neck," he said and handed the document to Amie.

After missing a considerable amount of the conversation between the governor and the Wampanoag, Amie and Damaris heard Prence say, "Philip, you must understand that we know what is best, and, trust me, it is not a good thing for you to give, sell, or dispose of any lands without our knowledge, consent, or appointment."

Damaris watched Phillip drop his arms, open his hands, and turn his palms towards the Governor in a show of compliance. "Today I pledge my desire to continue in friendship with the colonists, and I will not provoke war." Amie turned to Damaris and asked, "I wonder what he meant by that?"

"I'm not sure," Damaris answered. Her stomach flipped with guilt for holding back what her daughter had told her.

After Philip spoke those words he turned toward the door. He did not look back at the governor.

The governor began to say something more, then stopped, seeming to realize that his words would not be heard.

Philip's drawn lips softened and his squinted eyes widened when he became aware of his sister's presence. However, the deep red undertones of his brownish complexion took a little longer to lighten. When he approached Amie and Damaris, his thoughts seemed to be elsewhere, yet he stopped long enough for Amie to share with him why they were there and extend an invitation to the wedding.

"John Sassamon ran the land well," she said.

Near the bay, they noticed a shop with tall windows. Through the glass, the women clearly saw a nice selection of linen, lace, and other kinds of fabric that had been imported from Europe. Amie had saved enough wampum to trade for a wedding gift. They went inside where she and Damaris enjoyed the look and feel of the textiles. The colors were bright and the variety was overwhelming. Amie ran her hand over the elaborate vines intertwined in such a way that they formed subtle heart shapes combined with the floral pattern of this deep blue cloth, and then looked up. "What do you think?"

Damaris saw by Amie's expressive delight that she had found a treasure. "I think you have made the perfect choice."

Amie gave the shopkeeper the proper amount of purple and white wampum to pay for the imported fabric with its design that was intricate, intense, and ideal.

Chapter Five

❦Avoiding Tobias❦

Damaris

On their way back to Namasket from Plymouth, Amie tapped Damaris on the shoulder and pointed toward a trampled cornfield. "Here is where some cows and pigs got into my brother's cornfield, see, right over there." Damaris felt heaviness in her chest when she saw bent and flattened stalks, some with partially eaten yellow cobs dangling from half-bent plants. When she saw that the destruction repeated itself in patches, helter-skelter everywhere in the field, accompanied by the hoof-churned earth, she had difficulty speaking. "Oh, dear," she whispered.

"Oh, yes, Tispiquin told me that Philip got quite fired up about the devastation because the people who own the animals had refused to even up. Tispiquin said that Tobias put an arrow in one of the beasts as compensation and brought the meat back to the Wampanoag camp at Mount Hope." Amie's eyebrows came together, "I hope no more comes of it."

For much of the time, Damaris and Amie talked about wedding plans. Damaris felt her stomach churn when they came upon yet another landed estate that she was sure was still part of Philip's domain. "There seems to be an indefinite quantity of homesteads on lands that are the ancestral hunting grounds of the Wampanoag. Why does your brother allow the immigrants to use his land?" she asked, remembering the words of the governor to Philip about Plymouth having the power to control land deals. "Shouldn't settlers be working with Plymouth, not Philip?"

Amie's eyes flew upward, shaking her head from side to side. "Philip believes that he has traded these people temporary use. He should heed the warnings of the men in Plymouth." Amie's head dropped, then came back up, her mouth tightened. "You heard it, too. The governor tried to warn my brother that these people do not understand that he has struck a temporary agreement. Philip will expect them to vacate upon his return from winter camp."

Damaris looked again in the direction of the place and saw more construction. "I fear, by the looks of this house and barn, that these homesteaders think of themselves as the owners."

"Maybe Philip should have asked John Sassamon to go with him to Plymouth to have the town fathers write up these agreements so that both parties understand just what they are agreeing to," Damaris said. "John Sassamon understands that a well-written agreement will set things straight."

"If they did things that way, it would go on record and everybody would know exactly how things stand," Amie agreed. "Maybe Philip will listen to John."

Damaris rubbed her forehead in an effort to massage the stress she was feeling. "It seems to me that these new settlers are privy to special treatment from Philip."

Amie sighed and leaned against one of the larger trees that grew along the path. "The whole land thing is so tiring to me," she sighed. "Philip is willing to make his trades with these people because they give him the guns, gunpowder, and fire water that the Plymouth government restricts him from owning." Amie paused for a moment. "My brother trades with them because they pass around rum." After Amie made that statement she let out a sigh and said with hint of disgust in her voice, "I hate rum." She looked hard at Damaris. "It is a drink that Tispiquin is fond of from back in his whaling days. He drank rum aboard ship. He still does from time to time when it becomes available. I know Philip drinks it, too. It worries me because when our men get to drinking too much rum with the wrong people, they can make foolish land trades."

Damaris looked again at the homestead. "I can see why you are concerned about the strong drink. These people should not take advantage of our locals. Once they start to drink rum, they keep on doing it until they get to where they make fools of themselves." She looked at Amie and said, "Once in a rare while I can smell it on Jacob, but not very often. I smelled it on him the other day after John Sassamon's run."

"Philip says rum is a powerful medicine," Amie said with a twinge of disdain. "My brother sees no harm in these land deals, since he will not need these hunting grounds for a time." There was silence before Amie repeated her concern. "Philip and Tispiquin do not understand that it will not be easy for them to make the newcomers vacate when they are ready to utilize those lands again." She moved her hand in a slow sweep that drew Damaris's eye to perceive the vast lands that were still controlled by the Wampanoag. "It is my fear that these new people don't understand that our way of trading the use of shared hunting grounds is temporary. Philip will be very angry when he finds out that they will not be willing to move out."

Amie walked in silence until they neared the Wampanoag camp. "Let's spend the night here. I haven't seen my relations since the spring planting. It will be weeks before they head inland for winter lodge, and I will be able to invite them to Asowetow's wedding." She leaned back against a tree.

"Yes, let's. I'm glad for a chance to rest after Plymouth," Damaris agreed. She felt around in her side pouch. "This will be a good time to trade for wampum. I have a preference for the hand-drilled shell beads that your relatives make."

Amie agreed. "We are here at the right time to get a high-quality selection."

"Did you know that back in England they use silver coins instead of wampum to make trades?" Damaris smiled to herself at the thought of using coins for trading. "Hard to imagine, don't you think?"

Amie pointed to the pin that she wore on her over-blouse. "I remember a time when my people didn't know what to do with the shiny discs the English brought to trade. In winter camp, a few years back, I watched an Abenaki pound coins flat. He made this from one." Amie fondled the silver cut-out brooch on the yoke of her blouse and it caught the sunlight. "The Abenaki was a lone storyteller from the North." Amie pushed herself from the tree and stepped back onto the trail. "Have you met many of the Natives from the North? They are different from us. Some of them speak a different language. Him I could understand. He told us stories about how the bear lost his tail and why you might see a woodchuck up in a tree. He came to our camp in the middle of winter. He carried a most curious leather bag that held the most interesting silversmithing tools. He let us watch him pound out coins."

Damaris's eyes widened. "I've seen them. My parents had coins." She turned her ear toward Amie.

"He would say that what he did was his way to make good use of the otherwise useless coins. My friend Mary Uncas and I spent much time together watching him work the silver." Amie fondled her brooch. Damaris reached out and touched it, too. "He gave one to me and a matching one to her during the winter when the Mohegan were sharing our camp."

Soon the two came within view of the bark-covered domes of the Wampanoag.

Damaris glanced over toward the encampment and saw a Dutchman from up north speaking with Amie's older brother's councilman, Tobias, and other Wampanoag men. "It looks like the Dutchmen are trading."

There were guns, powder, shot, and what looked like blankets and shirts. About eight gallons of rum and two casks of beer were being traded for a high pile of furs and the precious quahog shells.

Amie reached out and grabbed Damaris by the arm, motioning to her to squat down. "It is enough raw shell to fill many canoes," she whispered.

They found a place to hide behind the brushwood. Amie's facial expression became blank and bloodless. "Tispiquin told me the demand has increased considerably, so it makes sense that they would come downriver to trade for the purple and white quahog clam shells." Her forehead furrowed and the corners of her mouth dropped at the sight of the stack of arms and ammunition that was displayed on the trade blanket. "Philip knows that it is the law from Massachusetts Bay down to Plymouth Colony: Indians who don't live in permanent towns under the colony's control are banned from owning guns."

"What would Governor Prence say if he knew that Philip's men are trading for firearms?" Damaris murmured to Amie.

Amie's shoulders went up at the same time as her hand covered her mouth. Wide-eyed, she whispered, "I don't know."

Damaris's stomach was tight and queasy. An inexplicable wave of dread pulsed from the top of her head all the way down to her toes. "What good is going to come from breaking the law?"

Amie didn't answer the question. Instead she pointed to the cornfields where the Wampanoag women were. "Look. I see Meetamoo. She is my relative."

Damaris and Amie glanced back at the traders and saw that they were engrossed in their transaction. Amie reached for Damaris's hand and nodded toward their clothes. "Look at us. We'll blend in. Let's go to Meetamoo." Damaris followed her as they quickly slipped toward the women in the field.

On the far side of a fallow field, Meetamoo was picking corn. She and others picked and tossed cobs over their shoulders into a woven basket carried on the back. The sweet cadence of the corn harvest song, "Lo ladi geah ah way ya hi ya way yo," drifted their way, and the familiar sound was calming. The moment Meetamoo looked up and saw Amie and Damaris heading their way, the chant began to fade. The Wampanoag women exchanged nervous glances before Meetamoo smiled to beckon Amie and Damaris over to the edge of the cornfield.

After Amie shared the news about her daughter's wedding, she began to speak to Meetamoo in Algonquin.

Damaris wondered if Amie had forgotten that she was able to understand every word Amie and Meetamoo spoke.

"They need the weapons to protect us from the loose animals destroying our cornfields. The old guns have been patched up so many times they can hardly be useful. Our men need new ones that work properly," Meetamoo explained. The other women stopped picking corn and stared.

Damaris listened to the lilt of the Algonquin language. So this explained the trading that was going on with the Dutchmen. She heard Amie promise Meetamoo that the secret was safe with her.

Amie took hold of Damaris's arm and turned her in the direction opposite the camp. "Adio," she said. They set out the longer way 'round.

"I will make it known about the wedding," Meetamoo called out after them. "I will tell your relatives."

The sound of the work song began to fill the air again as Amie and Damaris left the camp.

Chapter Six

❦The Midnight Hour❦

Damaris

Damaris returned to Namasket with Amie and saw that another six feet of height had been added to the cabin the local men were building for John Sassamon. They'd started it for their new preacher and were now finishing it for him and his soon-to-be bride. It was being erected over near the Council House about one hundred feet from the commons.

Damaris's eyes were drawn up toward the top of the construction. She took hold of Amie's arm as she watched Wannoo, Ephraim, and Wampye work together using a block and tackle to hoist a hewn log up to Jacob and Maskippaque. "It is not easy to watch my Jacob up there," she said, keeping her eye on the doings. She held tight until the churchmen set the support beam into place. "It's amazing what they have done so far."

"It is," Amie agreed. She pried Damaris's fingers from their grip on her arm. "They have made much progress." She rubbed her arm to get circulation going again. "I was not sure they would get the work done in time before the marriage ceremony."

Damaris turned toward Amie's ear. "Poor Sassamon has been camped in the council house ever since he arrived. I think he will enjoy this charming dwelling."

Damaris, exhausted from the trip, tucked Ruth in and settled into the feathers early. She had not yet drifted off to sleep when she heard the door latch move. "Jacob, is that you?"

"Yes, it is."

She pulled the linsey-woolsey drape aside and watched Jacob go directly to the woodbox, where he picked a good-sized log to place on the glowing bed of coals. He took the poker to the remnants of the fire. Sparks flew around and about the log, and soon the room brightened from the flames.

Seeing as he had done that, Damaris knew it meant that he would be awake for a time. She reached for her spun wrap and pried herself from the cozy nest. "How was your trip upriver?" she asked.

"Surveying is surveying." He sat in the rocker and moved his feet out towards the heat.

"Amie and I are amazed at the progress that is being made on Asowetow's cabin." Damaris stood behind Jacob, placed her hands on his shoulders, and began to put light pressure on the places she knew he liked. "It made me nervous when I saw you up there setting the beam."

Jacob leaned against her hands and fingers. "Ooh! That feels so good. Thank you."

Damaris stepped around to where she could see his face. "It was hard for me to watch. Weren't you afraid?"

Jacob motioned for Damaris to pull up a chair. "Maskippaque and I had quite the challenge to get the beam to fit in. It took us two tries before the thing seated right. After the roof, we are as good as done. The rest is up to John and Asowetow."

The glow of the fire brightened and dimmed as it reflected off Jacob, who glistened in the firelight. He had not taken the time to wash, yet, in spite of his manly odor, Damaris silently admired his fine features.

She gazed at her man and thanked God that Jacob was an excellent husband, dutiful father, and good provider. She had something heavy on her heart and felt a strong prompting from deep within her soul that willed her to enlighten Jacob about Philip and the Dutchmen. Jacob was trustworthy.

"Amie was able to invite Philip to the wedding," she said. "We talked with him when he was meeting with the Plymouth governor and the magistrates. He was there at the same time as Amie was registering." Damaris closed her eyes while her mind formulated the wording she would use. "The Rickard house is finished. Amie and I spent the night. The baby is good. She liked the blanket I made. It really is quite the place." A smile appeared when she stood up. "I think we could fit three or four of our little cabins in her big house."

Then her smile disappeared. "But I was ashamed at how rude Mary was about Amie. She almost sent her away, and to think it was all about everything that is going on with Philip and the Wampanoag these days."

Damaris waited for Jacob to say something or at least react, but he continued to stare into the flames of the fire, motionless and without expression. "Will this ever get better?" She stepped back in order to express herself with her hands. "That is where the trouble started. Mary's husband and the men he associates with at the tavern are all riled up."

Jacob poked the log.

Damaris moved the cast iron S-hook that held the bail of the teapot over the heat, then she continued. "I believe Philip and his men were in Plymouth because of what Amie and I saw on our way home. There was a field where the settlers' livestock had gotten into the Wampanoags' crops. There was a lot of damage done. Amie said that the loose livestock was the reason Philip was in Plymouth; to complain." She took a seat near Jacob. "The most unnerving thing that happened on our way home was when Amie and I were in the camp. We saw Tobias and others trading with Dutchmen for flintlocks and rum."

Jacob's brow furrowed. He rested his chin on his overlapped hands and leaned forward toward the hearth. "I need to mull that over."

In silence, husband and wife watched the log burn down to a gentle, cheery glow. Jacob reached for a fresh stick of wood. "Does Tispiquin know? Did Amie say that she would tell him?"

"The truth is, I don't know that she will tell him, because I heard her promise Meetamoo that she and I would keep what we witnessed confidential."

Jacob looked intently at his wife. "We can't let this terrible news ruin the celebration, but John Sassamon and Tispiquin will have to know about this. And it needs to be before long."

"Is there something you are not telling me? I see it in your eyes."

Jacob shifted his feet. "We were in the process of dragging the Gunter's chain on the road upriver when Francis heard a strange noise coming from the woods. We stopped what we were doing and went down through the gully and up the other side where we found a young fellow bound to a tree. The lad was about out of his wits telling us that he had been tied there for two days and two nights by River Indians."

Damaris felt the hair on her arms prickle. "Oh dear. How horrible. What would cause them to do such a thing to a boy?"

"He told us that they threatened to cut a hole in his father's breast and pull out his guts and cut off his head if his family didn't get off Indian land."

Damaris gasped.

"Don't worry, we took the lad back to his family." Jacob forced a reassuring smile. "Everything seemed fine. His father said that the River Indians passed through. He told us that his son was in the habit of fabrication and that the woodshed was next. Poor lad." He reached for the tea.

Damaris held her cup as steady as she could while Jacob poured the hot liquid. She was gazing at the small floating leaves when a wave of woe flooded over her. "I wish none of this had happened."

There was a rustle from the loft above and they saw their son Francis had awakened and was climbing down the ladder. "What is going on?" came the voice of a man.

Damaris could see her son's facial hair reflecting in the dim firelight. Jacob had been taking him along on the trips upriver to train his son to survey, yet she felt somewhat betrayed when Jacob called him over to become involved in their conversation. She wondered why Jacob did not send Francis back up to bed and spare him the worries of the outside world. Instead, she heard Francis ask, "Why don't the settlers build a cow commons like we have?" Before Jacob could answer, Francis asked, "Why are they living just one family here and one family there? How come they don't form into a village like us? For that matter, why doesn't Philip form a permanent village?"

Damaris was unaware that her desire to spare Francis the trials of adulthood was evident all over her face, until he stopped talking, looked at his father, and left the room.

Jacob's voice rose a bit. "Damaris, have you not noticed that I have been including Francis lately?" His perceptiveness was direct. "Remember, you are the one who encouraged me to take him upriver to learn to survey."

Francis came in with a chunk of dried salted meat that he had found in the hogshead. "Want any?" he asked.

Damaris shook her head, and Francis took a seat next to Jacob.

"John Sassamon is the one you should send to speak with Metcomet. John has a good way with words," Francis said. "He comprehends the tribal ways."

Jacob rocked the chair a few times, then straightened his back. His eyes went directly to his son. "The best outcome of that would be if Philip would become a Christian." He stood up, moved over to the hearth, and backed up to soak in some heat. "I don't understand. I can't count how many times John Sassamon has been over to Philip's camp." Jacob swayed back and forth before he sat back down in his chair. "Maybe Philip will never accept the message John Sassamon is trying so hard to share." Then Jacob drew in deeply before he sighed long. "Not even a preacher can make another person believe."

It had been a long day, and Damaris's heavy eyelids became difficult to manage, so she headed back to the feathers. She listened to the two men discussing the issues. Jacob and Francis continued to analyze King Philip's options, their voices echoed into an otherworldly realm and she drifted off to sleep, leaving the current events unresolved.

Chapter Seven

✦The Wedding✦

Damaris

It was a beautiful day. The maple trees displayed the glory of the Creator's paintbrush. Damaris gazed at the leaves as they rose, fell, and lifted this way and that on the branches. A current of air blew through that caught the corner of a greenish-red leaf. Damaris watched it spin 'round and 'round before it broke loose and fluttered to the ground. A rain cloud slowly moved across the way. It briefly caused a shadow across the path that led to the council house. The grass that framed the path glistened and danced in the gentle breeze that moved the dark cloud on its way to the east of the wedding assemblage.

Tobias, Wampapaquan, and Mattashunnamo, the same three men Amie and Damaris had seen trading with the Dutchmen, appeared in the shadow of a mature chestnut tree. Their faces and bodies were painted and tattooed, their heads adorned with feather clusters tied to their hair, and they were wearing newly sewn leathers and moccasins.

They were joined by King Philip, whose hair was decorated with wild turkey and split eagle feathers. Half of his face and the shaved area above his forehead had been painted crimson. His naked chest and arms showed off dark blue tattooed designs. He was bright and colorful, like the dancing fall leaves that gloriously reminded Damaris of the season's change.

She looked again and saw that there were now six Wampanoag men. Their inked skin, red face paint, quill sheaths, and neck knives, plus their handsome display of wampum belts and feathers, caused them to look spectacularly unapproachable.

The local folks from Namasket, Middleborough, and many of Amie's relatives had turned out. Damaris counted at least eighty people. She imagined they were as grateful as she was that the missionary John Eliot was there to officiate. It was only befitting, since he was Namasket's first minister and the groom's mentor. He was in extraordinary physical condition for his age, likely due to all the travel required in making his rounds. He was devoted to the thirty-three growing Christian Indian villages that he had established between the Bay Colony and Plymouth.

The weather permitted the witnesses to gather outdoors in two rows, creating a path for the bride and groom. All came, except the now nine warriors from King Philip's camp, who remained in their agglomeration under the chestnut tree. One of them was wearing a red riding coat, the very one that had been on Amie's wall. It came to life on the frame of the aged but well-preserved body of the sachem Tispiquin. The sun reflected crimson from his well-oiled, black skin. He had wrapped about him a four-inch-wide red, green, yellow, and dark blue hand-woven sash, tied so that its tassels hung down to the right of his waist.

When the proceedings outside of the council house were about to begin, Tispiquin and his brother-in-law, King Philip, left the now thirteen warriors standing in silent enforcement beneath the ancient tree.

A striking, self-confident woman stepped from the tree's shade. She was dressed in the old traditional-style deerskin dress that had only one shoulder covered and the other left bare. She came over to stand near Amie, who turned towards Damaris. "This is my brother's wife, Woo-tonekanuske." Amie spoke in English before she turned to speak Algonquin, telling Wootonekanuske "Mittamwossis, Damaris." She then went on to explain that she and Damaris had been friends since they were little girls.

Damaris gave a nod and smile to Wootonekanuske.

Amie also wore a deerskin dress. She had on a fresh linsey-woolsey overblouse trimmed with some of the blue fabric she'd had left over from sewing Asowetow's wedding bodice. Front and center was her silver brooch.

Damaris heard Mary Sipit whisper to Amie, "Joseph and I are delighted that John Eliot has come to perform the ceremony. He has been very good to us." She smiled at Woo-tonekanuske and then turned to Damaris and whispered, "If it had not been for John Eliot, Joseph and I would still be under the power of Philip. At our age we are so thankful that we do not have to move and camp four times a year."

"Look, I see them." Damaris felt a wave of anticipation wash over her. She pointed out the bride and groom to Mary Sipit. John Sassamon, straight and tall, was dressed in a fine wool doublet and new beaver felt hat. She could see by his unchanging smile and beaming eyes that he felt blessed as he approached the gathering with Asowetow on his arm.

The bride's skirt was unique and beautifully fashioned of lightweight red wool. Her chemise was made of fine imported linen and trimmed with lace. The bodice she wore was fashioned from the blue fabric that Amie had purchased from the shop at Plymouth. Damaris thought it was perhaps the first of many fine dresses Asowetow would wear. After all, she was getting married to a minister who was also a cultural ambassador. Asowetow was more than capable of fulfilling her obligation to assist John Sassamon in the duties of his ministry to the Indians as well as the colonials.

The bride kept her eyes on her man as she passed her wedding guests. She did not look to the east where her father was and she did not look to the west where the women were.

As Damaris witnessed John Sassamon and Asowetow's radiant joy, a scripture came to her mind from the book of Jeremiah. "Thus saith the Lord; I remember thee, the kindness of thy youth, the love of thine espousals, when you wentest after me in the wilderness, in the land that was not sown." Her thoughts of love for Jacob welled up from deep within, to the point she found it necessary to wipe away a tear. The couple walked past to take their stand in front of John Eliot. Damaris peeked at Amie as she witnessed her daughter and John before the Reverend, and wondered if her dear friend was feeling gain or loss.

Everyone turned their attention to John Eliot, who raised his hands and motioned for the congregation to be seated.

Damaris made herself comfortable in the grass between Mary Sipit and Ruth. She looked across at Jacob, her son Francis, and the other men. "I am blessed," she thought, and took hold of her daughter's hand when John Eliot began.

"*Neenawun.*"

"We are gathered here today."

"*Wunumau a missimin noh matta aonk wussuwongganit matchetou, asuh matta neepauook, ummayeuoit matcheseanuog, asua matta apegk wutappuoganit mamanowontamwarnin.*"

"Blessed is the man who does not walk in the counsel of the wicked or stand in the way of sinners or sit in the seat of mockers."

"Qwuttinoowaonganit Jehovah wuttapeneaumouonk, kah wuttinnoowaonk missantam kesukodtacu kah nukkonieu."

"But his delight is in the law of the Lord, and on his law he meditates day and night."

"Kah ogqueneunkqussu mehtugqut ahketeamuk ut kilhke fepupogqut, noh ummeechummounk uppauntunk nehenwonche uttoowutchu: kah ooneepog matt apish missegn."

"He is like a tree planted by the streams of water, which yields its fruit in season and whose leaf does not wither. Whatever he does prospers."

Damaris noticed that King Philip listened intently to every word that Reverend John Eliot was speaking in Algonquin to the couple about God, love, and covenant.

Later, at the wedding feast, Damaris witnessed King Philip purposely sit next to Missionary Eliot and become engaged in what looked like an enthusiastic conversation.

John Sassamon made his rounds. He spoke with a cluster of guests and moved to another group. When he came to Philip and John Eliot, Damaris watched in awe to see him drawn into their discussion. She felt her heartbeat throb in her ears when Jacob and Francis moved to join in the exchange with them. "I will inquire of Jacob later," she told herself. She rose to rejoin in the women's work and to track down Ruth.

She discovered that her daughter was watching a game with other children. The boys had formed two equal teams for a game of double-ball. They had selected two-and-a-half-foot smooth sticks and were using two tightly sewn leather sacks that had been filled with corn seed. The sacks were connected by a leather thong. They had set up a goalpost on either end of the meadow. The object of the game was to pass the double-ball from stick to stick and run towards the goal. If the ball got tossed over the opponent's goal post, the team scored.

Ruth intently watched young Peter pass the double-ball over to Philip's son, Ninigit, who enthusiastically gave the leather sacks a fling over the goal. All the children on his team cheered.

When Damaris finally got Ruth's attention, she gave a hand signal to inform her where she could be found after the game.

Damaris watched the children at play. They had become more skilled at the game since the last gathering. She only saw the migrant children once or twice a year. The changes in their development seemed dramatic compared to the local youth, whom she saw every day.

Just then, Ninigit ran past with his stick held high, ready, should the ball be passed his way. Damaris could not help thinking of King David's son Absalom in the Bible, because the boy had a most magnificent head of hair. She was amused to think back at how out of proportion his thick mane had looked in comparison to his small frame of years past. Now his body was proportionate to his hair.

Damaris continued on her way. How beneficial it would be if Philip would leave the migratory children here for the winter, where they could study with John Sassamon and have the opportunity to learn to read and write.

As she approached the cook arbor, the smell of smoke mixing with the aroma of roasted meat caused her mouth to water. Mrs. Tinkham had taken charge of the women volunteers, who tended a large spit and kettle.

"It looks like our men have outdone themselves with the provision of meats," Damaris said when she saw that, even though the other guests had eaten, the women were still cooking.

"There will be enough duck, turkey, venison, and bear left over for everyone to be able to bring some home," Mrs. Tinkham said.

Damaris saw that the clay vessel of cornmeal pudding she and Ruth had brought earlier had already been moved over to the side of the cooking coals, where it was staying warm. "Do you think anybody will even want some of this? Maybe I don't need to serve it."

Mrs. Tinkham lifted the lid of the Dutch oven, gave the contents a stir, and replaced the lid. "Last week's harvest festival and today's eats are almost too much of a good thing."

Damaris smiled. "It is nice that each family brings their own trenchers and other eating implements so that there is not going to be a great deal of extra cleanup. Someone needs to make sure the leftovers are taken home by the guests."

"I will go," Mrs. Tinkham said. She hung the ladle on the side of the fire irons and headed over to where the guests were gathered. The announcement echoed over the crowd in Mrs. Tinkham's empowered voice.

Damaris noticed that the ashes needed to be cleaned from the base of the outdoor clay oven where the bread had been baked. Thankful that she didn't have to yell in public, she happily peeled off her clean overdress, put on an apron, and set to cleaning the oven.

Amie found her there. "My Asowetow is married. I know he is older, but they are so well suited."

Damaris rose up from a small cloud of ashes and wiped her face and hands with her apron. "What matters is that she truly loves him. I was brought to tears when they walked by. Did you see the way they looked at each other?"

The corners of Amie's mouth and the glow of her eyes revealed the extent of her satisfaction. "Asowetow liked the fabric we bought in Plymouth. She wants to use some of it to adorn their four-poster."

Damaris picked up the insinuation Amie had made and kept her composure. "I hope they live long and give you many grandchildren."

———— ❧ ————

Jacob and Francis were engrossed in a conversation with John Eliot, Anthony Naughton, who was visiting from another praying town, and King Philip at the time Damaris and Ruth decided to leave. They passed by the chestnut tree where Philip's men were in a powwow with Tispiquin. His red coat stood out in contrast to their glistening, tattooed upper bodies.

Damaris instinctively drew Ruth close as she watched Tobias's finger point towards the east, then to the south, and sweep back around.

Damaris chose a path for herself and Ruth that avoided passing the chestnut tree on her way to say their farewell to the bride before leaving. She found Asowetow surrounded by well-wishers. Damaris waited her turn before she put her arms around the new bride and gave her more congratulations. She took her aside and whispered, "Being married to someone in such an important position as John Sassamon is not going to be easy. If you ever need to talk to someone, I am here for you." Damaris stepped back, then leaned in to Asowetow's ear again. "Anytime. Remember that." Damaris looked into Asowetow's eyes to be sure the girl understood, before she stepped back from the newlywed and put her arm back around Ruth. "You will make each other so very happy."

***

Ruth warmed some leftovers. "The molasses you brought back from Plymouth made our corn pudding taste delicious."

"Molasses like that is a treat." Damaris savored its unique sweetness. "The kind of treat I save for a special occasion."

Ruth became quiet and deep in thought. Damaris dozed. The fire died out and the room began to chill.

Damaris's own snort woke her and Ruth up and she realized the men had not yet come home. She laid up a small fire and watched it brighten behind Ruth's head, creating a halo by means of the wild hairs that had freed themselves from the child's braids. "They played double-ball very well today," Damaris said. She gazed at Ruth's heart-shaped face. The flicker of dancing flames drew her into a thought that she had not expected to come so soon. It had been hard enough to accept the fact that her son, Francis, had become a man, and now Amie's nephew Ninigit was doing the same. "How old is Ninigit?" she wondered. "Twelve or thirteen, perhaps." The thought forced Damaris to come to terms with the fact that Ruth was fast approaching that fine line between child and adult. "You may as well enjoy the games now, because, before you know it, you will be required to work with the women." She tried to stop herself, but she felt it necessary to find out if Ruth was drawn to the Indian boy. "Asowetow's cousin Ninigit played well today."

Ruth's eyes brightened. "Were you watching when he caught Tohanock's toss and made the goal?"

"It was a spectacular catch."

Ruth straightened her back and turned toward her mother. "Ninigit had quite a few good runs."

Damaris wished life could be as simple as Ruth's game. And presently she saw no pressing reason to tell her daughter that she and Amie had seen the elders trading for muskets at the Wampanoag camp. What good purpose would it serve to say anything negative to Ruth about the boy's father? Any day now Ninigit would be going with the Wampanoag to trek inland for the winter. "John and Asowetow have asked for permission from Philip to keep Ninigit over the winter so that he can learn to read and write, but, last we heard, his father told them no."

Ruth lifted her eyes to her mother for a brief moment and then her attention went back to watching the dancing of the flames.

Damaris sat in silence for some time before she asked Ruth an unusual question. "Do you know what it means to be equally yoked?"

"Yes. It is when two oxen are the same size and they fit in the yoke perfectly. That way they can pull the load straight and not go crooked or cause the other ox to stumble. Why?"

"I want you to understand. John Sassamon and Asowetow are very different in some particular ways. They are very different ages. Her father is from another country and her mother is Wampanoag, so she is a mix. John Sassamon is from the Massachusetts tribe. He is not Wampanoag. However, even so, they are equally yoked. Do you know why?"

Ruth's shoulders rose up and her forehead furrowed. She looked up at her mother, "No. Not really."

The corners of Damaris's mouth lifted. Her eyes softened, "They are loved by God, they belong to Jesus, and because of this, they are sealed by the Holy Spirit. They are both Christians. A person's differences do not matter if they are both Christian. This is what it means to be equally yoked in the faith." She reached across to Ruth and placed both of her hands on the girl's shoulders. "Will you make your mother a promise?"

"What is it?"

Damaris looked into her daughter's eyes. "Promise me that when you marry, no matter who that person is, you will marry another believer."

They leaned in toward each other, hands and eyes locked. "I promise."

In that moment Damaris felt a peace about Ninigit and thanked the Lord for such a blessed answer.

Ruth headed off to bed, so Damaris busied herself with the spinning wheel. She pedaled her wheel, the hum hypnotic. She pulled the wool and gazed at the graceful movement in the hearth. Her thoughts drifted to the work that went into making candles. There had been just enough of the precious beeswax stowed to last the winter as long as no one burned candles frivolously. She had lit one anyway, because she knew that the men were discussing matters of utmost import. The glow of the candle and the whir of her wheel were a comfort as she waited up for her Jacob.

Finally the wooden latch moved, and Jacob and Francis came in simultaneously. Damaris slowed down her spinning while Francis stoked up the fire that brightened the room. "When I left to help with the cleanup, I noticed you talking with Philip." She snuffed out the precious candle. "What were you menfolk talking about so intently?"

Francis's eyebrows raised. The corner of his mouth curved upwards by the power of puberty. "I heard him say to Sassamon that he best better enjoy his new-made bride while he can," Francis told.

Damaris's eyes opened wide and she raised her fingers to her mouth, "Who said that to John?"

"Philip, Amie's brother," the two men answered in accord.

She settled back and took the wool back into her hand. "John Sassamon won't go over to Philip's camp right away. He is not quite finished working with John Eliot on the Indian language texts." The pedal began its up and down motion again. "In a few weeks he plans to finish the translation and get the script over to James Printer at the Nipmuck village. John Sassamon told Asowetow and Amie that the grammar needs some work before the text is ready for the typesetter." Damaris continued to work the wheel at a rhythmic pace. "What else did you menfolk have to discuss?"

Jacob took the fire poker and lifted the bottom log a bit to allow the air to circulate and cause the flames to come back to life. "It's just like you said, the settlers' livestock is getting into the Wampanoag corn and Philip is up in arms." When he pulled the poker back, the log dropped, giving off a flash of light accompanied by cinder sparkles. "He asked us if we truly believed that Plymouth would be able to protect them from this ever happening again."

Francis took hold of a green switch and attempted to ignite its tip by poking the point between the logs where there was a red glow. "We heard Sassamon agree to spend time this coming winter in Philip's camp, teaching him to read and write so that Philip can express himself better to the Plymouth magistrates." The tip of the stick began to catch a flame. He put the flame out and lit it again and again.

"I don't think Asowetow was very keen on it. You should have seen the look she gave her new husband."

Jacob reached over and put a stop to Francis's fidget by gently taking the twig from his son and placing it in the fire. They watched it flame and create billows and swirls of smoke.

Francis asked, "Would you want to spend your first winter alone if you were just married?"

Damaris blushed, "Not likely."

Francis's eyes twinkled before he smiled and brought up his hand to cover his exaggerated cough. "Ahem."

Jacob tilted his head, opened his eyes wide, and directed his puppy-like expression toward Damaris. He brought his hand to his chin and said, "Hell, no."

Chapter Eight

❧The Unexpected Visit❧

Excerpt from the writings of Damaris Cooke,
1677 Massachusetts.

As the years passed it seemed like everything around me was changing. Even Asowetow began using her English name of Betty. By and by, more moved here from near and far. They also came as more of Philip's Wampanoag were hearing and believing the good news about Jesus. I give much credit to the tireless efforts of John Sassamon, John Eliot, and the Naughtons, who continued to preach to the Natives. The fact that Philip was allowing his son Ninigit to spend time with the Sassamons was encouraging to me as well.

Middleborough had grown to the point that the colonials moving into the area had been building bigger houses and had even built a new Congregational church that looked much like the one in Plymouth. Amie wanted to go and check it out just to see what it was like inside, but I don't think she ever did. Jacob and I went over to it once with the Tinkhams, but we never intended to leave our simple council house on the Namasket side of town like the Tinkhams did.

December 1674

Damaris

Damaris was alone in her little cabin enjoying Jacob's "Tinkham" rocker when suddenly there was a quick knock before Betty Sassamon came in with a burst of sunlight, wind, and snow. "Damaris. Damaris. Are you in here?"

"Yes, I am here." Damaris watched the minister's wife dust the snow off her wool cloak and stomp it from her high-top moccasins. There was a long period of awkward silence. Damaris assumed Betty was waiting for her eyes to adjust to the room. She watched in the firelight as the snowflakes melted one by one in the highs and lows of Betty's wavy hair.

From the way Betty was fidgeting with her muff, Damaris suspected there was something troubling her. This might be a time she should offer the pastor's young wife some tea. "You look cold," she said. "Let me make us some tea to warm you up." She fished out the precious porcelain cups that her mother had brought over from England. "How are Ninigit's studies coming along?"

Betty glanced around for a chair. "That is one of my concerns. He had just begun to study, then, of a sudden," she found a seat on a chair near a small table, "Philip sent for Ninigit's return. I thought you knew? This happened last week."

"I knew he had gone back to the camp, but I was not aware this was to be permanent." Damaris poured the hot, black birch beverage.

Betty shifted herself this way and that on the chair. She brushed at snow that was no longer there before her eyes fell on Damaris's outstretched hand holding the cup of tea. "Do you remember what you whispered to me on my wedding day?" She cleared her throat as she accepted the tea. "That I can talk to you about…anything?"

Damaris prayed to God that she would be able to have the wisdom to help Betty with whatever her concern was. "Yes. You know you can come to me with anything and I will not pass judgment."

Betty's dark-complexioned face flared up with deep red undertones. Her long, black eyelashes fluttered. She lifted her hand to her lips. "It's about my husband." There was a considerable pause. Just when Damaris was about to say something to help move things along, Betty spoke again. "Are you sure we are alone?"

"Yes. We are alone. Jacob and Francis went ice fishing and Ruth has gone over to see the new baby at the Tinkham's."

Betty's eyes gave the room a quick investigation as if to make sure what Damaris had said was true before her timid reveal. "John came home from Philip's camp last night and he did not want," she looked down toward the floor and shifted herself again in the chair. "I was clean and scented." She blushed. "Just the way he likes." Betty looked directly at Damaris. "That is not like him. I mean. He always wants. He always wants my attentions, especially if we have been apart for any length of time."

Damaris poured herself more tea. "Did John have anything to say about his trip?" She studied Betty's face to see if there was any indication that Betty might be feeling distrustful of her husband and found none. "Did John have anything to say about why Philip wanted to have Ninigit brought back?"

Upon hearing the last question, Betty stood up with her cup in her hand and paced slowly back and forth in front of the fire. "He never said a word to me as to why. The boy was doing very well with his studies. Not only that, but I could tell that Ninigit was happy to spend the winter with John and me." Betty's begging eyes demanded to have an answer. "Many times when my husband comes home from spending time with Phillip he has been moody, but not to this extent. Lately not only does he sit for hours staring at the fire without speaking, he has not been about his sermon preparations as he should."

Damaris watched as Betty moved about in front of the hearth. "Do you think it is because some people are visiting the new church in Middleborough? Or perhaps something went wrong while he was at Philip's camp?"

Betty set her teacup down with a bit more force than Damaris would have liked. Tea splattered about. Betty's hands went to her hips. Her plump, well-rounded lips tightened. "I'm sick of it," she said through her teeth. "The 'big King' has something that is not right going on over there, and I think that is what is eating away at my dear Sassamon, and I don't know what it is."

How bad had the situation gotten if John was not responding to Betty's obvious charms?

The girl sighed. "Philip is not going to change. My husband goes over there to Philip all the time. It seems like he is at King Philip's beck and call. Every time I ask him about it, he says to me that maybe this will be the time that Philip will pray to Jesus and bring his people to Namasket. We had hopes with Ninigit. Well, it's never going to happen as far as I can see." She paced and turned toward Damaris. "Do you know what that Philip said to John Eliot at our wedding?"

"No."

"Philip pulled on John's button and told him that he wanted to be a Christian just about as much as he wanted that button. That's what he said to John Eliot." Her eyes begged Damaris to respond. "Nobody talks to John Eliot like that."

Damaris's heart sank at the words she was hearing. She reached over to the shelf and retrieved the worn, leather-bound Bible. "Jacob reminded me that it isn't up to us to make someone believe. We can give them the gospel message and that is all we can be expected to do." She thumbed through the book of Mark. "Even Jesus himself has said not everyone is going to believe. Ah, yes. This is the part where Jesus was teaching his disciples after he told the parable of the sower. 'The sower soweth the word. And these are they which are sown among thorns; such as hear the word. And the cares of this world, and the deceitfulness of riches, and lusts of other things entering in choke the word, and it becometh unfruitful.'" Damaris closed the big book. "We need to understand that God must give people's hearts the choice to believe. Philip wields a great deal of power over the people he leads. If they become Praying Indians he will lose his control and the tributes he receives. Philip is in a struggle and he does not see a good future for himself if he gives all that up in order to settle in one place."

Betty's face seemed to soften. "I understand what you are saying. My John simply can't blame himself."

Damaris set the book aside and rose to take hold of Betty's hands. "Nobody here doubts that your faithful servant of a husband has gone above and beyond to preach the gospel accurately to Philip. And now all any of us can do is to trust God to fulfill His purposes."

Betty's shoulders lowered and she sat back down on the chair and picked up her cup. "My husband has no reason to blame himself." She drained her cup and rose to leave. "Now if only I can convince him that he has done all that he can possibly do. He needs to let go. He needs to release Philip into the hand of God."

Chapter Nine

❧Jacob's Unexpected Trip❧

Excerpt from the writings of Damaris Cooke, 1677 Massachusetts.

After Betty's visit that winter's day, things began to settle and get back to normal. The following Sunday we received a sermon about accepting the Lord's will. I felt that it was John Sassamon's way of letting us know that Ninigit's visits had been cut off indefinitely.

From time to time the following year, John Sassamon made pilgrimages to visit King Philip, but they became less and less often.

January 29, 1675

Jacob

It was a snowy morning. Jacob was outside the cabin chopping wood when Betty came running over to him from across the way. "Jacob," she said, "John has not returned from his trip to Plymouth. It has been over a week since he left Namasket to meet with Governor Winslow. I expected him to come home days ago."

It was more the strain in Betty's voice that caused a pulse of dread to pass through his gut. He put down his ax. It was not like the minister to be gone this long without sending word. He straightened up his pile of wood before he rose to say, "I will go straight away to see about it."

Impulsively, Betty threw her arms around him and he noticed tears running down her cheeks.

"Oh Jacob, thank you so much," she said again. "Thank you."

By this time, Damaris had heard the commotion and stepped out onto the porch.

Before she had time to ask, Jacob said, "I must go and prepare Barge for a ride to Plymouth." He pulled his wool coat together and tightened it. "I will be needing some dried meat and hardtack." Jacob turned and headed toward the barn, his mind full of travel details and worry.

———— ◦◦◦ ————

The snow along the trail was cumbersome. It slowed Barge. The moon was high overhead by the time Jacob arrived in Plymouth. When he found his daughter's home, he decided to wait until morning to disturb his son-in-law, Mary, and the children. He led his horse out to the back where the horse stable was.

Jacob wiped down the horse and got himself settled down in the hay.

He heard voices outside. He strained to make out what they were saying. The dialect was Algonquin, but the accent was different than at Namasket. He understood enough to make out what they were talking about.

The two debated their plans to pass through Plymouth. Jacob lay still in the livery. He continued to listen. The river Indians settled in for their night's lodging.

Jacob could barely make out the images of two men as they stealthily entered the barn and set themselves down in the hay on the far side of the barn from where he and his horse were resting. He quietly breathed a sigh of relief that they did not seem to be aware of his presence.

Jacob's ears perked when the strangers began to discuss the body of another Indian they had found drowned and wedged under the ice at Assawompsett Pond. They had discovered the dead body with an ice-fishing pole and waterfowl lying nearby.

The taller silhouette said, "The hunter must have drowned."

The other seemed to agree. "We did the right thing. It was only right to have given the poor soul a burial." The short one then asked, "Should we report the death to the officials since we are in Plymouth?"

His companion said, "They have no notion for a dead Indian. Indians are our own responsibility, not theirs."

"I agree. We needn't delay our trip. Let's just move on."

"Before sunup."

Jacob's heart pounded when he recalled the lad who had been tied to a tree. He waited for what seemed like an eternity before he was sure the upriver Indians were settled.

He shivered. Should he ride back to Namasket right away to look for a new grave near Assawompsett Pond? He had not asked around the township for John Sassamon, yet. There was no reason to think the dead Indian was Sassamon. He deliberately slowed his breathing. Most likely Sassamon was just delayed here in Plymouth. He'd search the town tomorrow.

With that in mind Jacob settled off to sleep.

Jacob woke to bright sunlight streaming through the cracks in the walls and was relieved to find that his company had already left. He got up and brushed off the loose hay. He washed his face in the trough, watered and fed his horse, and then approached the house, where he found his daughter's family at the board.

Mary let her father into the kitchen through the back way. "Father, come in," she said warmly. "Join us for breakfast."

The neatly dressed children were quietly staring at Jacob with big eyes as they ate. Suddenly one of them said, "Grandfather, how come you have funny hair?" There was laughter and snickering among the siblings. Another one said, "You're not our real grandfather. Our grandfather would not wear dirty Indian clothes."

At that point, John Rickard rose from his chair, lifting the back of his hand in a gesture of discipline. The children quickly silenced themselves. "Show your grandfather some respect."

Later the men retired to the library. John Rickard loaded a long-stemmed clay pipe with some tobacco and handed it to Jacob. He did the same for himself and lit them. "The children are not all that out of place," he said through a cloud of blue smoke. "You are a frightful sight."

Jacob drew long and hard on the thin tube, then blew the smoke out slowly. "I did not take the time to clean up because we have a concern for the well-being of our pastor, John Sassamon. Have you seen him around Plymouth?"

"Yes, he was here last week." John Rickard broke off the tip from the stem of his pipe and threw it into the fire. A few sparks flew. "A fella at the tavern was saying that Sassamon came to town to warn Governor Winslow about Philip. Word has it that Philip is endeavoring to engage all sachems 'round about in a war." He re-lit the pipe. "Josiah Winslow didn't think much of the news and sent John Sassamon on his way." John Rickard puffed. "I myself don't trust Philip, Tobias, or any other of his councilors. And I'm not the only one." His face reddened. He looked at Jacob with slit eyes. "There are quite a few of us around here who think he is a filthy heathen, and the sooner we can put a stop to his devilment, the better." He stood up and paced by the fireplace. "And you and Damaris," John's eyes bore into Jacob while he paused, "don't you know why we don't bring the children up to see you?" His tone rose. "You live with the stinkin' savages. Just look at yourself. You even smell like one."

Jacob prayed to God that he would not let loose a punch at his son-in-law. "I'm leaving now to go see Governor Winslow."

John took the pipe from Jacob. "You can tell that Indian-lover, Winslow, that he is a fool to trust his damn King Philip. He is going to find out that he has been trusting a snake."

Jacob took a long walk in the snow along the ridge in an effort to settle his nerves. He looked down at the wharf and could see two well-built ships. One was unloading pineapples, sugar, and other goods from the Caribbean. The other tall ship was unloading passengers. In other places on the docks were stacks of furs, tobacco, and other cargo from the colonies to be loaded for the return trip to England. On the shore were local citizenry who stood huddled in the cold, anxiously waiting to welcome their friends and relatives into the colony. Their happiness caused Jacob sadness. He turned towards the Governor's office.

Jacob felt more comfortable with Josiah Winslow over former Governor Prence because they had grown up together. Josiah's father was one of the first governors of Plymouth and one of the first allies of the Wampanoag. While Jacob waited to be called, he thought of the red riding coat Damaris and Josiah's fathers had gifted Massasoit.

Jacob waited to hear the words "come in" before he opened the heavy door to the governor's office.

"Jacob, my friend, good to see you." The governor's voice was robust. "How is that pretty wife of yours?"

Jacob took a seat across from the governor's desk. "She is doing fine." He took a deep breath. This was no time for idle chatter. "I'm here because we are concerned about our pastor. John Sassamon's wife is beside herself. John came here to see you last week and has not yet returned home."

"Oh yes, yes, he was here." Governor Winslow leaned back, then forward. "I confess, I did not take the man seriously. He seemed like he was overreacting to something he'd heard."

Josiah shifted himself in the hand-carved chair that had once belonged to Governor Carver. "Philip and his men came here not long ago to turn over his rifles and promise peace. Tobias and Mattashunnamo presented the arms with a great deal of pomp and circumstance." The governor's bristled brows came together. He raised his hand to his chin. "I have been thinking about that Indian preacher ever since he left last week. He was acting oddly and said that he feared for his life if he were to get caught. He said that Philip was amassing arms and stirring up the surrounding tribes."

Jacob slumped over, put his face in his hands, and rubbed his eyes. "I don't like the sound of this. Do you know if John Sassamon is still in town? Has anyone said they've seen him?"

"As far as I know, he left for Namasket right after he talked with me."

"Josiah, I'm afraid for Sassamon." Jacob's heavy lids dropped closed. The thought of the boy tied to the tree, the angry words, *Cut a hole in his breast, cut out his guts, and cut off his head* played in Jacob's mind. He felt guilt in his own gut for not defending the poor boy who had been taken out to the woodshed for a beating. As much as he had tried to tell himself that the youngster's story was made up, deep down he had suspected that the boy was telling the truth. Jacob told the governor everything he had heard in the livery. "Assawompsett Pond. I heard them say Assawompsett. That is right where John Sassamon lives. If John left Plymouth about a week ago, we have to go check out the River Indians' story."

The corners of the Governor's mouth drooped to a full frown. He sat silent for a time before he responded. "It looks to me like you better go see if what you overheard pertains to your preacher." The two men stood up simultaneously and shook hands. "Let me know if their story has any substance."

Chapter Ten

✤The Investigation✤

Jacob

When Jacob came home, he found several Namasket townsmen as well as a few men from nearby Middleborough engaged in a discussion in front of Amie's house. Tispiquin raised his hand and motioned for Jacob to join in the powwow. "Wannoo thought he recognized John Sassamon's fishing pole by a hole in the ice. There was blood but no sign of a body, unless you count two dead ducks."

Jacob's stomach churned as he told the group about the River Indians. "I heard them say that they had pulled a bloated body out from a hole in the ice and buried it somewhere in the embankment." His heart ached inside his chest. "I have tried to tell myself the body was that of a stranger. Just someone passing through."

The pink and yellow horizon was a reminder that the February day was drawing to end, yet the anxious Namasket men stood around. From inside Amie's abode could be heard the somber sound of women doing their best to console Betty. Jacob moved in to where he could address Tispiquin personally. "Governor Winslow is sending a deputation to look into this. We can't be sure it is John Sassamon without a body."

The next day, Wannoo guided the townsfolk to the ice-fishing hole. Tispiquin and Jacob were accompanied by Middleborough's Constable Jabez Howland. Eventually they found the hole about forty-five feet or so out onto the pond. They followed signs in the snow that indicated more than one person had been coming and going from the place in the ice for fishing. The hole was frozen over about two inches thick. Next to that was John Sassamon's fishing pole and two duck carcasses. Jacob squatted down and picked up a lure in the shape of a fish carved from quahog shell and another one made from bone. "It's all here." He picked up the pole and ran his hand down the short, flat, fire-hardened shaft, and looked up at Tispiquin. "Just like I heard the River Indians say."

"This is Sassamon's. I recognize the lures."

The solemn group doubled back, following a blood trail and drag marks that led them to a possible burial site on the embankment.

Constable Howland stepped forward with his spade and attempted to move the dirt, but the frozen ground made his work difficult. He had apparently started at the head of the body, as his work exposed an ear. Although John Sassamon dressed in the manner of Englishmen, he had always worn a silver hoop with a ball and cone in his right ear. Tispiquin said, "The earring looks to be John's."

Jabez dropped to his knees and began the work to carefully remove the dirt about the bruised and swollen face. "I believe this to be indeed John Sassamon's body," the constable announced. He pushed himself up and walked directly over to Betty, who stood staring at the partially exposed head. "Mrs. Sassamon." He took her shoulders into his hands and shook her gently. "Mrs. Sassamon. Can you identify this person as your husband?"

Betty took a long time before she turned and examined each one of the faces in the group. "My John was a good fisherman. He would never fall into an ice-fishing hole." Then she looked intently at the constable. "Something bad has taken place and I want you to find out who did this to my husband." She stood there with no facial expression and eyes like stone. "He should have listened to me." Betty's voice was monotone. "I begged him not to go to Plymouth. Before he left the cabin, he said that he was worried for his life, and now he is gone. Gone."

Betty addressed the remains of her husband, quavering, "Why didn't you listen to me?" She dropped herself to the ground and lay upon the grave, silent, for she was spent.

Wannoo put his hand on Jacob's arm to get his attention. "It can't be. To kill John Sassamon, our pastor, make no sense. John has much respects."

Jacob put a gentle, brotherly arm around Wannoo. "Yes, much respects."

Jabez replaced the dirt over John's head as best he could. "I shall straight away go to Plymouth to deliver my report."

The townsfolk followed Constable Howland back to town.

Damaris

Amie and Damaris remained behind to support Betty in her grief. They could hear bits and pieces of the conversation going on among the departing entourage. *He was too good a hunter to do something stupid.* Damaris's feet were feeling uncomfortably cold, yet she stood still and listened to the words being carried by the natural acoustics of Assawompsett.

"Who would…to kill…?" asked Wannoo.

Tispiquin's voice chimed in, "…River Indians. Jacob, tell us again what you heard them say." And then the voices faded away. She could not make out any more.

Damaris got down on her knees and Amie joined her to pray over Betty and the soul of her dear husband. Damaris spoke, saying, "He was a believer and we know he is with our savior. Blessed Jesus has welcomed John Sassamon home. He gave his life in the service of God. We can trust that the very moment he died his soul came into the presence of Jesus."

Amie rubbed Betty's back. "Our precious savior has already welcomed John into glory, saying, 'Well done, my good and faithful servant.'" She put a little pressure on her daughter's back. "Look at me. You know what I'm saying is true. It's all right to grieve. It hurts. We're still here and we need to release our heartbreak."

When Amie and Damaris had finished with their words, the three stood arm in arm by the gloomy grave. Amie broke out with a plaintive chant. The tones eerily echoed round about. Betty chimed in with her mother, and after the third round of the vocables, Damaris caught the concept of the lamentation. The wailing put her in mind of the Biblical description of the professional grievers at the death of the daughter of the leader of the synagogue in the book of Mark: *And he cometh to the house of the ruler of the synagogue, and seeth the tumult, and them that wept and wailed greatly.* Damaris let out unfettered emotional vocables and felt a sweet release as she joined in with her loved ones in their strange crying. They lamented for a long time. It wasn't until an unusual, algid wind came and went through their huddle that they ceased their lamentation. The coming and going of the strange wind was as if Sassamon himself was giving them permission to take their leave.

On the way home, they walked in silence until Betty turned to her mother. "I don't want to leave him there. As soon as the ground thaws, we are going to have John Eliot over to give my husband a Christian burial."

"I agree. He needs to be moved to the cemetery as soon as the ground thaws."

"As soon as the ground thaws."

Chapter Eleven

❧The Cause of Death❧

Excerpt from the writings of Damaris Cooke,
1677 Massachusetts.

The news was spreading throughout the colonies. The people around the many praying towns were speculating about John Sassamon's death and what had happened at Assawompsett in Namasket. Some were wondering if he might have fallen into the ice-fishing hole and frozen before he could get himself out. Others were convinced that he must have suffered an accident or, worse yet, been murdered by King Philip's guardians. There was a great deal of discussion going around about King Philip and what could possibly be a logical reason that would cause him to wish the death of John Sassamon.

March 1675

Damaris

Damaris and Jacob were awakened by a loud clamor outside and rose from their featherbed. Jacob was the first out the door. "What is this all about?"

He was followed by Damaris, wrapped in a wool shawl. She watched from the porch. There was a cluster of men gathered around Constable Jabez Howland and the coroner from Plymouth. The two were the center of attention. An oxcart stood ready with a wagon loaded with shovels. "We are going to exhume John Sassamon's body, and the coroner here is equipped to do an autopsy."

Tispiquin came out from across the way and so did Amie and Betty. They watched from their porch. They looked curiously at the men on the road and then over to Damaris. Jacob stepped down to talk with Jabez and returned with his mouth tight and eyes set firm. "Step aside, I'm going with them." He went inside to change.

Francis came down from the loft and, having heard what was going on, said, "I'm going."

By the time Jacob and Francis came out there were more volunteers: young Ephraim Tinkham, Tispiquin, Maskippague, Wannoo, and many others followed the wagon.

The women, joined by Ruth, watched Jacob and son hasten to catch up with the workforce that trudged toward the thawing grave at the edge of Assawompsett.

When Damaris waved, Amie and Betty wasted no time in coming over. Damaris stoked up the fire underneath the kettle.

Betty's once deep-brown sheen had an underlying achromatic tinge that served to emphasize the deep-felt grief she had endured. "Does anybody know what the coroner plans to do, or when I will be able to give my John a proper burial?" she asked.

Damaris poured her a cup of tea. "I'm not sure what is going to happen. A coroner is like a doctor. They are trained and have a way of looking the body over and by doing a few tests they can determine how the person died."

Betty sat down next to her mother. "I hope this testing will not take very long and we can get on with giving him his proper burial. Where do you think they will be taking him?"

Damaris answered, "Most likely they will take him to the Council House. It is early in the day, so they might even be able to give us an answer today."

Amie put her arm around her daughter's waist. "Then we can lay him to rest."

Damaris warmed up some three-sister stew. "You will not be good for much if you don't eat something. Please have some sustenance."

After the anxious women had finished eating, they wondered how many hours they would have to wait. Amie looked at Damaris's wooden box that held her English things. "Let's look through your treasures and show Betty what your parents brought over."

"Yes, mother, let's," Ruth piped up. "I have not seen your things in a long time."

Damaris was relieved that Amie had come up with an idea that would keep Betty's mind occupied. Each thing she took up from the box had a story she could share. There was a tiny blanket that her mother had wrapped little Oceanus in. "My mother was expectant when she boarded the Mayflower. It took longer to get here than anyone had anticipated, and the baby came while they were still at sea. She named him Oceanus because of it."

Betty took the blanket in her hand. "I never heard you speak of him before."

Damaris reached for the blanket and began to fold it tenderly. "He died shortly after he was born." Ruth put her hand out for the little blanket, and Damaris passed it to her. "You probably didn't know that I also lost a sister during their first winter. I never knew her, either. They both died before I was born. Her name was Damaris as well. She was ten years old when she traveled here with my parents." She pulled up from her box a small girl's skirt, bodice, and little white coif and handed them to Betty. "These were hers once. They named me after her." The clothes had never quite fit her perfectly.

"My sister Deborah and I wore these when we were her size. The last girl to wear it was my baby sister Elizabeth." Damaris grew more doleful. "My mother experienced difficulty in giving birth to little Lizzy. That is when Mother became quite ill. Neither one of them were quite right after that. It fell on me to care for them and run the household back when we lived in Plymouth."

Amie reached out to take the garment from Betty and ran her hand over the worn, blue wool. Her eyes lifted. "You were wearing this when I first saw you. What age were we then?"

"We were in our tenth summer," Damaris said.

Later in the day, the waiting women dozed until they were awakened by Jacob and Tispiquin. "We need more candles." Jacob was already moving Damaris's box aside so he could get at the candle stash. "The coroner only has a few more tests."

Betty rose and took hold of Tispiquin's arm. "Father, what did they find out?"

Tispiquin shook her hand away and stepped back. "No water in his lungs. The coroner says that this means John did not drown."

Jacob straightened up with a handful of candles. "Not only did he not drown, it looked as though he was involved in a struggle. His face and neck were badly bruised."

Betty stepped back, her focus directed towards her father. "I warned him not to go. Did I not tell you Philip had something to do with this?" She turned to Amie. "All because of the implements of war." She glared back at her father. "My uncle killed my husband over arms."

Tispiquin appeared to grow large. He drew air into his ample chest. Jacob went out on the porch with the candles and Damaris busied herself straightening Jacob's leavings. Amie, with her elbows out and her hands on her hips, stepped between her husband and daughter and, with squinted eyes focused on her daughter, she brought two of her fingers up to her lips, signaling for silence. She paused to take in a breath before she spoke. "Betty. We do not know that to be true. They are still investigating. We will have our answers soon enough."

In the Council house, John's body had been laid out on two benches pressed together to make a serviceable table.

Wannoo watched the coroner turn the body on its side, move the head, and open the mouth to use a medical instrument. It took many hours for the coroner to inspect every part of John's body, reading subtle signs to determine the cause of death. When he was done, the coroner carefully moved John's arms across his chest and draped linen fabric over him.

The coroner frowned at the body. "This death was not an accident. If we find the killers, we may need to show the judge the body. But who knows how long that will take?"

"Wannoo know way to keep John." Wannoo explained how he'd seen the weak left to hibernate during the winter when he was younger. "Keep safe."

The natives agreed with Wannoo so the coroner allowed that it might work. "Then we can give him a final burial after the trial."

Wannoo supervised as they wrapped John Sassamon in a linen cloth and placed him in a bark receptacle that they lined with sphagnum moss. They also used the moss to pack the body tightly before they placed him in a temporary grave lined with bark. They covered it with more bark panels and placed chunks of ice on top, then more moss.

Wannoo whispered a prayer over the pastor's grave. "Creator carry Sassamon to your place of beauty." Then he sang a haunting chant to assist John's soul to the spirit world.

———— ✤ ————

At the Cooke cabin, Jacob was tossing and turning in bed, causing Damaris to finally throw the feather cover aside. "What is the matter with you, Jacob?" she asked. "How am I to get any sleep with your thrashing around like that?"

Jacob rolled to face his wife. "I can't make any sense of Sassamon's death." He shifted so his head was better supported. "Over and over, I think, *this was no accident.* But why? It has to be the guns. I cannot come up with any other reason for them to do this atrocious thing. The constable has taken Tobias, Wampapum, and Mattashunannamo into custody to be put on trial for the murder." Jacob swung his legs around and sat on the side of the bed. He bent forward to support his head in his hands. "Governor Winslow made it clear that he wants me to be present at the inquiry."

Damaris got out and walked around the end of the bed, pushed the curtain aside, and sat next to Jacob. "What if the rumors are true? What if Amie's brother, King Phillip, really did have something to do with this murder?" She put her arm about his waist.

"I know," Jacob said. "I can't stop thinking about what you and Amie saw going on with Tobias trading for guns at the Mount Hope camp a year or so ago."

Jacob stood up and headed to the wood box. Damaris watched him build up a small fire. He looked back from the hearth. "The way I see it, John Sassamon may have seen new activity going on while he was at the winter camp," Jacob said.

Damaris looked across the room at her husband's furrowed brow and began to shudder and sob. "I have so wanted to believe that Amie's brother would not want trouble. Now, I'm very worried."

Jacob returned to the bed and enveloped Damaris in his arms. "I am, too," he said. "I don't know if our towns will be safe if this thing escalates."

Chapter Twelve

⚜Pre-Trial⚜

Excerpt from the writings of Damaris Cooke, 1677 Massachusetts.

In the days before the trial, a heavy, quiet gloom hovered over Namasket and Middleborough.

Jacob

Jacob was in his rocker when he felt the subtle vibration of someone approaching. He was up and out of his chair and had his hand on the latch of the cabin door before Wannoo had the chance to knock.

Wannoo's black eyes moved this way and that. He looked over his shoulder to see if he was being followed. "Wannoo have want to talk."

Jacob nodded and he stepped back to let his Indian neighbor in, offering him the rocker.

"Winslow, he want me to be to the jury at trial." Wannoo unfolded an official paper and handed it to Jacob. "Take three of King Philip's men to make stay to Plymouth. Tobias for one." He shifted and began to rock forward and back. "To be true, I be good for that." he said. The momentum of the chair increased. "John Sassamon die. Wannoo fear Wannoo next die." Wannoo stopped mid-rock and leaned forward. His long braids fell toward Jacob. The whites of his eyes were in stark contrast to his brown skin when he blurted out a confession: "Wannoo not give King Philip wampum pay in four winters." Wannoo's lips drew tight, then he let out a sigh. "Tispiquin, he pay to King Philip and Plymouth. Indians in praying town, John Sassamon, and John Eliot say we stay in Namasket, pay to Plymouth, not Philip. Plymouth now need protect Wannoo."

"That is how I see it," agreed Jacob. "As a praying town, we are under the protection of Plymouth."

Francis came in from the back with an armload of wood. Wannoo rose to depart saying, "Plymouth paper come for six praying Indians. Paper say sit on jury."

"I will be there; and Ephraim said he will as well," Jacob said. He watched his son drop the armload of wood into the box by the hearth.

Francis brushed a lock of hair from his forehead and looked toward Wannoo. "You can count on my father and me to be present for the Court Session."

Jacob stood and walked behind Francis. He placed his hands on his son's solid frame and squeezed his shoulders. "You can count on this fine young man to accompany us, as well as young Tinkham."

Jacob came out to the community garden where Damaris, Ruth, Amie, Betty, and some of the other women of Namasket were at work with their rakes. The women stopped what they were doing and gathered around Jacob. "Jabez reported everything from the coroner's inquest to Governor Winslow."

Betty looked sharply at Jacob. "Did he say it was Philip? John told me he feared Philip."

Jacob motioned for Betty to sit down. He reached out with his arm and lowered his body to the grassy knoll. "After investigating the area, Jabez determined that three men had sneaked up behind and grabbed Sassamon by the back of his head and twisted him around." Jacob paused and picked up a small pebble and began to roll it around between his fingers and thumb before he looked at the dead man's wife. "John put up a good fight. By the way it looks, the struggle was over quickly." Jacob sighed and dropped the stone. "What I want you to know is that John did not suffer very long before he died. The coroner's autopsy results indicated he died of a broken neck."

Betty picked up the little stone and examined its quartz vein. "Thank you, Jacob, for telling me personally." She carefully put the little pebble in her leather bag that she wore about her neck and wrapped her hand around the pouch. "Philip's men murdered my husband. What is the governor going to do about it?" Her eyes were intent. "I want justice."

"Some argue we should turn the three culprits over to King Philip to handle the matter because John Sassamon was an Indian," Jacob revealed.

"Absolutely not." Betty pulled so hard on the pouch that the thong almost broke.

"What we know is that Tobias, Mattashunannamo, and Wampapaquan have been arrested and are being held at Plymouth. They will go on trial in Plymouth when the next General Court convenes. There are six Indians who have been asked to be on the jury."

Damaris

A few days had passed when there was a knock on Damaris's door and in came Amie, eyes wide as she spoke with velocity. "Damaris, Tispiquin is gone to Plymouth to post bail for Tobias. He intends to sign over two square miles of our Namasket land."

"I'm sure that Plymouth will not release the prisoners, not when their guilt in the matter is in question." Damaris attempted to reassure her friend.

"If they accept his offer, Tispiquin will be responsible for Tobias. I couldn't stop him from going and now I don't know what to do." Amie's breathing was quick and shallow. "I don't want to have Tobias at our house. He gets Tispiquin worked up and confused." She glanced this way and that and moved her feet constantly as she explained. "Tispiquin told me that he believes in their innocence, but I am not convinced." Amie rubbed one hand over the other. "To be honest, Tobias frightens me. Betty is so upset with her father right now, she won't speak to him. She has holed up in her cabin and won't come out."

Damaris's heart beat rapidly. Her own face began to flush. "I don't blame her one bit. I'm terrified."

Chapter Thirteen

❧ The Verdict ❧

Excerpt from the writings of Damaris Cooke, 1677 Massachusetts.

The day of the trial finally came. At first, Amie wanted to stay at home; the talk of it being a murder committed by her brother's trusted councilors was upsetting to her. But Betty was set on going and seeing justice served, so Amie agreed to come for her daughter's sake. I was feeling much the same as Amie: I wanted to go and I didn't want to go. In the end, I brought Ruth along so that she could babysit Mary's children. Mary was set on going to support her husband, who was on the jury.

Ever since John Sassamon's death, Mary had been reaching out to Betty. The two of them rekindled their childhood friendship. It was good to see Betty have a safe place to stay while Tobias was her father's charge.

When Amie, Betty, Mary, and I arrived at the trial, I was amazed at how many people were crowded about inside and out of the courthouse. We were able to find a place up in the balcony. There were just about as many Indians in the gathering as there were Englishmen. I could see my husband Jacob and my son Francis sitting up towards the front of the large room. Ephraim Tinkham was with them. Tispiquin was between the Namasket men and Philip's Wampanoag. It seemed strange to me to see Governor Winslow sitting in a prominent position on a podium, only because I remember Josiah when we were growing up. He chased me around with a dead bird, threatening to put its beak up my nose. The day of the trial, Josiah looked very important dressed in his robes. Behind him was a jury of twelve Englishmen and six of our Namasket Indians dressed in their best. Wannoo had cut his braids.

Damaris

The bill of indictment was read:

"At this Court three Natives were arraigned, vizs, Tobias, Wampapum, and Mattushannamo, for that being accused, that they did with joint consent, upon the 29th of January, anno 1674, at a place called Assowamsett Pond, willfully and of set purpose and of malice aforethought, and by force and arms, murder John Sassamon, another Indian, by laying violent hands on him and striking him, or twisting his neck, until he was dead; and to hide and conceal this their said murder, at the time and place aforesaid, did cast his dead body through a hole in the ice into the said pond."

Damaris could see that all eyes were on Jabez Howland. He brought his fisted right hand up and placed his thumb and forefinger on either side of his Adam's apple and cleared his throat. The buttons of his vest strained against the pressure caused by his expanding belly. He drew in a deep breath and began his opening statement. "Let it be known that John Sassamon had reported to Governor Winslow that he witnessed King Philip amassing arms."

Damaris's toes curled in her moccasins when Jabez glanced over in the direction of the governor and the jury box. "John reported to the governor that Philip was making preparations to make war upon the English." She glanced toward Amie. Her friend stared at Tobias, and looked deep in thought. She wondered if Amie was thinking about that day they witnessed the same three men trading for arms. Her thoughts were jarred when Jabez turned his attention toward the crowd. "John Sassamon feared for his life."

Governor Winslow raised and lowered his head in agreement with what he was hearing.

Then Jabez turned his head to face Josiah. "Isn't it true, Your Honor, that Sassamon came to you, Governor Winslow, to forewarn the colony that King Philip and his men were amassing arms with the intent of joining forces with the Pequot, Narragansett, and others to come out against us?"

"Yes, indeed, this is true." Governor Winslow's eyes fell upon the three accused men. "John Sassamon did come to meet with me to deliver said message and he also told me that he feared King Philip's closest defenders, Tobias, Wampapaquan, and Mattashunannamo, that they might be sent to destroy him if he were to report what he saw them doing."

Jabez paced back and forth while he spoke. He cleared his throat again. "After a thorough examination of the body, the coroner has determined that John Sassamon's death was not an accident but that he was indeed attacked. They broke his neck and then his dead body was forced into the ice hole." He looked again at the Governor. "At this time I would like to ask permission to bring the body of John Sassamon into the courtroom."

The entire room erupted with sighs and sounds of shock and dismay at the thought of a body being brought in as evidence.

Damaris could see that Betty's face had lost its red undertones. Upon noticing that John Sassamon's wife looked gray, she was about to offer to take her out of the courtroom when Amie took Betty by the arm and bent down and whispered in Damaris's ear. "The poor, dear girl doesn't need to witness this. I'm taking her outside. Don't you miss one thing. I want to know every single thing that happens."

"I promise," Damaris said, and watched her friends make their way through the crowded room and out the door below. She was able to spread out a bit before someone else quickly took their place.

"Quiet, please," Winslow said firmly.

The room settled into a stark silence when the coroner and two other men carefully opened the elm bark container. They unpacked the insulation and placed the wads of moss into large baskets and bark buckets as well as the chunks of ice that had been keeping the body preserved for so long.

Once the body was exposed, Jabez picked up a two-foot rod and cleared his throat.

"At the inquisition we found that John Sassamon's neck was broken by twisting of his head around." He pointed out the neck injury. "We found that the body was extremely swollen, with lacerations and contusions in several places. We also found that no water issued out of the body, which indicated to us that this victim, John Sassamon, the beloved pastor of Namasket and Middleborough, was indeed murdered."

The assemblage began to murmur among themselves to the point that the Governor had to call for order in the court before Jabez could continue.

Damaris felt her heartbeat intensify when she heard Jabez call the name Jacob Cooke. Her cheeks felt warm when her husband stood up to testify about what he had overheard the River Indians talking about in the horse barn.

"I heard them say that they had come upon a dead body that was under the ice of a fishing hole," Jacob told. "The two River Indians were discussing with each other about how they were uncertain as to what to do with the body they had pulled out of the ice-fishing hole." He looked at Jabez before his eyes turned to Josiah. "I heard them say that they had felt that it would be proper to show respect by giving the dead Indian a burial, as was their native custom."

"Thank you, Mr Cooke. You may be seated," Josiah said.

Jabez then said, "May it please the court, I would like to call the accused."

Damaris flinched when the older woman who had taken Amie's place took hold of her arm. Tobias stepped forward.

Tobias drew himself up, shoulders back, his chin tilted upward, and his eyes glared hard in the direction of Jabez. "This thing was none of our doing. We sent Sassamon home with the message that King Philip did not want a war with the English."

"That is not true," came a voice from one of two Indian men standing over by the door. The Governor motioned for them to come forward, which the men did.

"State your name." Governor Winslow motioned for the one who had spoken to come closer.

"My name is Patuckson, sir."

"Please approach the bench."

Before letting go of Damaris, the woman whispered, "He is from another praying town. Perhaps he knows something."

Damaris nodded. "Yes, I know who he is."

Everyone in the room began talking, to the point that the Governor had to drop the hammer. "Order in the court." There was an instantaneous hush. Everyone waited for what would come of this. "We have an eyewitness."

After the two Indian men had placed their hands on the Bible and sworn to tell the truth, he indicated for Patuckson to reveal what he saw happen.

Patuckson stood motionless, holding in his hands a fine coat that was beautifully embroidered with moose hair. "The day the murder happened, I was standing behind a tree on a hill near the shore of the pond where the attack on Sassamon took place. These three men did violently assault and murder Sassamon. And they tried to conceal their crime by throwing his body through a hole in the ice, making it look like an accidental death."

Tobias's eyes tightened and his face reddened. He blurted, "His story is not true." He raised his finger and pointed to the coat in Patuckson's hand. "This Patuckson owes us a gambling debt."

Patuckson's eyes grew large and his mouth dropped open at Tobias's words. "No, look here at this coat." He brought the coat forward as he was speaking. "They gave this to me because they wanted me to conceal the murder that they had committed."

Tobias interrupted, "That is not true. Patuckson had played away his coat, but we returned it to him, not to keep him quiet, but to demand instead the payment of his debt in the wampum that was agreed upon. Instead of paying us back the amount that he owes us, he is now accusing us." His lips tightened before he looked directly at the Governor. "He only wants you English to think of him as a better," he paused, "Christian."

At that moment, William Naughton, the other Indian who was with Patuckson, came forward and was given permission to speak. "Before John Sassamon left Plymouth, he had said to me that he feared King Philip, Tobias, Wampapaquan, and Mattashunannamo."

Tobias's voice rose a decibel, "We did not murder John Sassamon. His death was an accident of his own account."

Jabez walked over to Tobias and led him up to the corpse to point out the evidence of the broken neck when all of a sudden the corpse moved on its own. John Sassamon's head flopped to the side. The mouth of the corpse dropped open and the body began to bleed afresh from his eyes and the lacerations as if it had been newly slain.

The sight of this grotesque phenomenon caused the entire room to erupt into a frenzy. Damaris's mind began to spin. The woman who sat next to her screamed out, "Oh God!" before rushing away.

As sick as she felt, Damaris stayed. Mary did, too. They could see that the Governor had all he could do to regain some sort of order with those few who were still in the room. He ordered Jabez to bring Tobias up to the body one more time. The corpse began to bleed again from the wounds.

An Englishman on the jury shouted out, "It's a sign."

Another voiced, "It's an omen. They are guilty."

Then other jurors said the word, "Guilty." The others joined them in unison saying, "Guilty" over and over, until most of the people who had stayed in the room joined the chant. "Guilty. Guilty. Guilty!"

June 8, 1675

The verdict was read as follows:

"We; of the jury, one and all, both English and Indians, do jointly and with one consent agree upon a verdict: that Tobias, and his son Wampapaquan, and Mattashunannamo, the Indians, who are the prisoners, are guilty of the blood of John Sassamon and were the murderers of him, according to the bill of indictment."

Chapter Fourteen

❦The Execution❦

Excerpt from the writings of Damaris Cooke,
1677 Massachusetts.

During the trial, Mary and Betty became close.
Mary was as glad as Betty was to see the accused
come to trial. Betty refused to go back to Namas-
ket. As much as I wanted her to come back home for
her mother's sake, I couldn't blame her. The Native
women usually enjoy more of a voice in their homes
than we colonial women do, but not in the case
of Tobias. For whatever reason, Tispiquin went
against the whole town's advice when he brought
Tobias here. We all felt a great deal of endanger-
ment during the trial and the week of the execution.

Betty and my Mary devised a plan where Bet-
ty would take the role of Mary's personal servant.
For as long as each of them was getting something
they needed from the arrangement, it was probably
a good thing.

That is when I began to think of how I might
protect Ruth if trouble were to come. Our family
friends in Massachusetts Bay Colony kept coming
to mind. Thomas's mother had taken ill and was in
need of assistance. Jacob and I made plans to bring
Ruth there for an extended visit. Ruth was getting
to an age where she could indenture for a year or so.

This was the most sensible alternative that we could think of for her safekeeping should the need arise.

———⚜———

June 8, 1675

Betty

Betty caught the brim of her hat as yet another stranger bumped into her. There was no space for apologies. The crowd formed to watch the execution.

More than just the locals had come to see the spectacle. Uncle Philip's Indians and some Narragansett and Pequot hung around the fringes of the massive crowd.

Her mother, Damaris, and Mary were there with her, making their way through the dust and heat, past the barking food vendors. The smell of unwashed travelers, oiled Indians, and burned baked goods made her choke.

They found shade to the right of where the gallows had been erected. Their menfolk were in a cluster on the other side. Betty had seen them earlier, but now that people were merging in closer, a tall, plump lady blocked her view of them. "Can you see my father?" she asked.

Mary rose up onto her toes and looked. "No, I can't see him. He's not with Jacob and Francis." Then she gestured over toward the fringes. "Wait, I think I see him with the Indians over that way."

Betty's lips tightened. Better to be a servant than to return to her father's household when he sided with her husband's murderers. "Does your offer of refuge still stand? I'm more than willing to help out with little Mary and the others, that is, if you truly meant what you said last night."

"Oh yes," Mary smiled and took hold of Betty's hand. "I truly meant it. You would be a great help to me."

"Now that we have given my husband a Christian burial here in Plymouth, this is where I want to be for a while." Betty pulled loose of Mary's hand and turned in the direction of the churchyard graves. "I feel the need to be near him." Then she turned in the direction of the gallows. "God forgive me, but I hate my Uncle Philip, I hate my father, and right now I hate them all for what they did to my John." She addressed Mary again. "Maybe someday, by God's merciful grace, I will be able to forgive them, but today, all I want to see is justice served."

The sound of drums could be heard in the distance and grew louder as the procession came toward the gallows. Betty could not bring herself to look at the convicts when they were marched past, but she could hear the voice of the minister, John Cotton. "Repent. Turn to Jesus. Confess your sins! Turn and be saved. Jesus is just and good to forgive no matter how bad you have sinned."

Betty watched the preacher plead with the three men who were about to be executed and felt as though she was as guilty before God as they were. John Cotton was preaching directly to her. Still, she would not repent, and it looked like neither would the prisoners, because they had hardened, defiant expressions on their faces. Her teeth clenched and she experienced a sick sense of sweet justice when the noose was placed around the neck of each of the three unrepentant murderers.

The whole time John Cotton did not stop asking them to repent and confess before God.

For Betty, justice was coming and she might at least be able to feel some satisfaction. When the blocks were kicked and the bodies dropped, silence ensued within the crowd. Betty repented and said, "Lord, forgive me for I have sinned." It was as if the Lord was saying, "I have heard you Asowetow, and you are forgiven." With that, her entire body felt a flood of unexplained peace.

Meanwhile, amidst the creaking of strained ropes, Wampapaquan's noose broke and his traumatized body dropped. His eyes blinked several times before he shook himself, began to rub his neck, and lifted the coiled sisal noose. Betty watched him take in air, a great deal of air, before he tossed the thing with its frayed ends off the scaffold. "I repent," he cried. "I didn't do it. They did it."

The red-faced son of Tobias took in a great deal more air before he pointed to the swinging corpses. "They murdered John Sassamon. I was there, but I didn't do it. I just watched, that's all. I didn't do it," he cried.

A man's voice rose from within the crowd. "It's a sign. He's innocent."

The courtyard erupted with loud voices. Some were saying, "Hang the devil again," and some were saying, "Let him go."

The magistrates decided not to hang Wampapaquan again, so Constable Howland took him into custody in order for the powers that be to decide what they would do next.

The minister, John Cotton, walked along with Wampapaquan. "Jesus gave his life so that men like you can be forgiven," he explained.

Chapter Fifteen

⚜Tispiquin's Mystique⚜

Jacob

In Plymouth, a layer of dust settled on the throngs of people who had come to witness the disturbing executions. They had camped for far too long. Jacob watched in relief as the horses and wagons clogging the narrow roads began to head off in different directions. If only this was the end of the whole mess.

He walked with Damaris and Amie over to where Wannoo, the Sipits, and the Tinkhams were saying goodbye to their hosts, the Rickards. He rested his hand on Damaris's arm. "I think I will stay the night."

He turned toward Amie. "Did Tispiquin say if he was heading out today or tomorrow?"

"I do not know. I have not seen him since he left to speak with Josiah Winslow about Wampapaquan." Amie's eyes glanced toward where Betty and Mary were. "If Tispiquin brings Wampapaquan back to Namasket, or not, Betty will want to stay here."

Jacob placed his hand gently on Amie's shoulder as their daughters exchanged a weak smile. "Time will heal. Give her some time," he said. Then he moved closer to Mary. He wanted assurance that his daughter's motives were noble in wanting Betty to stay. He had seen Mary and her husband at their worst, and not that long ago. What had changed?

"I'm glad we were able to make it work," he heard Mary say. "It was Betty's idea. I never would have thought of putting all the women and children in the house and having the men bivouacked in the livery."

Mary looked lovingly at the group from the Namasket praying town. She smiled warmly at all: old, young, Native, and colonial. "You have opened my eyes as to how Jesus wants us to live," Mary said to the eclectic group.

His daughter took the hand of the older native woman, Mary Sipit, and said, "Thank you so much for the deep conversation we had."

Betty chimed in. "Oh, yes," she smiled at Mary Sipit. "You taught me things about Jesus that I didn't know, and I am a pastor's widow."

His daughter and Betty Sassamon would do fine together, Jacob decided with a wave of relief. His Mary had turned back to the beliefs he had taught her. He smiled fondly at her and turned his attention back to his own goodbyes.

Maskippaque and Wannoo stood apart from the others. Their eyes darted from side to side as if expecting an ambush. He wanted to say words of encouragement but found it difficult. In his long silence, thoughts of the trial and executions repeated in his mind. They'd been on the jury. Why were they still unsettled?

"Wampapaquan heard the words of John Cotton and repented," Jacob assured them, not knowing for sure if that was what had made them anxious. "Tispiquin should be allowed to bring him to Namasket."

Wannoo spoke. "Tispiquin a good man, skillful. He have powers. He no die by fastball."

Maskippaque and Wannoo exchanged a glance. "Tispiquin have warrior ability." Maskippaque's lips tightened and his forehead furrowed. "He not like John Sassamon to have power to speak for us."

Jacob placed his hand on Maskippaque's shoulder and gave a smile. "Tispiquin should do fine with Josiah." Then his smile grew into an all-out chuckle. "Now tell me all about how come Tispiquin is invincible?"

Maskippaque's eyes got big when he looked at Jacob in disbelief. "You no hear how Tispiquin become our Sagimo, receive red coat, marry Amie?"

Jacob could see that he had opened the door for one of their stories, so he motioned toward a place in the grass where they could sit.

Maskippaque closed his eyes, dropped his head, and was silent before he lifted it back up, opened his eyes, and began the story. "Many moons ago, when I was young, Massasoit brought us to camp on the seashore. I was rolling string of unfinished wampum shell in groove of sandstone. I see far out to sea where water and sky put together." Maskippaque paused and made a hand visual of the arch in the horizon. "Out of nowhere there appear a ship, big against the sky. That ship have many sails. My eyes see ship grow large. The closer ship come, the bigger it get. At first, we run hide in bushes. Later we learn ship called the Potvis. There come to shore many men from lands far away. They give gifts. There be much trading, big dance, food. One man from ship, he be Tispiquin. Tispiquin, he big. Tispiquin, he black. Tispiquin, he strong. Tispiquin, he win challenges, he win respect from Massasoit, and he win Amie." Maskippaque looked at Jacob and Wannoo to see if they were still paying attention.

Wannoo let out the vocable, "Heh heh."

Jacob said, "Go on."

"Tispiquin have one turtle's back of time before he be let free from captain Goltzius's indenture. Then he have Amie for wife. She wait the long year for Potvis to return.

Amie, she long for Tispiquin. Amie come clamshell beach. Amie, she wait, Amie, she watch for whaling ship, Potvis, to carry Tispiquin.

Then one day Amie she see ship. Tispiquin, he come ashore, tell Massasoit he now free to marry daughter.

Maskippaque's face scrunched up in such a way as to look fearfully angry. "Captain Goltzius hear Tispiquin say that he be done with whaling. Captain Goltzius order sailors take Tispiquin back to ship."

Maskippaque paused.

"Heh heh."

"Go on."

"Sailors be told tie Tispiquin to foremast."

Maskippaque's face relaxed and his eyes lit up with joy. "Tispiquin, he break loose." Maskippaque quickened. "Tispiquin, he strong, like Samson." The storyteller's eyes grew large, and his hand with its pointed finger moved in the direction of the bay. "Tispiquin, he jump ship. He swim. Sailor men fire guns. Many shoot. Ball hit Tispiquin. Ball from big guns bounce off. Tispiquin no can die by lead ball. Tispiquin safe with Massasoit. Massasoit make Tispiquin sachem, give Tispiquin much land, give Tispiquin Amie. Give Tispiquin red coat."

Maskippaque turned his attention toward Wannoo as if to ask if Wannoo thought he had left any of the details out, and Wannoo said, "Tispiquin have much ability." His eyes flashed toward Jacob before his eyes, mouth, and head dropped. Then Wannoo turned his attention to Maskippaque. Maskippaque nodded in agreement before Wannoo said, "Tispiquin no have tongue like Sassamon."

That evening Jacob was alone with John Rickard in the study. John lit a clay pipe for Jacob and himself. "Jacob, I believe I owe you an apology." He drew in and then slowly let the smoke curl upward from his parted lips. "You were right when you told me that the aboriginal people of this land can be made civil." He looked toward the ceiling and brought his hand to the bowl of his pipe. "I never in my life thought I'd see Indians in a courthouse serving on a jury, and I have to say they handled themselves very well." His eyes grew large. His bushy brows rose. "The Indian, Patuckson, the one who came forward and testified, was articulate."

Jacob looked directly at John and slowly drew long on his pipe before he spoke. "The one you would have been impressed to listen to was Betty's husband." He reached up to wipe away the unexpected moisture that formed in the corner of his eye. "Her husband, John Sassamon, could preach."

———

Days later, Jacob woke in Namasket. He pushed aside the bed curtain, slipped his feet into his moccasins, and stepped outside. He stood on the porch in his limp nightshirt and felt the stillness of the fall morning that was in contrast with the turmoil within himself. John Sassamon had not only been a friend, but also a dependable mediator between the colonials and Philip's Wampanoag. The loss weighed heavier after listening to Maskippaque and Wannoo's concerns about Tispiquin's lack of diplomacy. Should he stay home in case there would be some kind of repercussion from Philip over the trial and execution?

Across the street, the scrimshaw piece that Amie placed in her new glass window was still there. She was in the habit of leaving Tispiquin's scrimshaw in plain view, as a sign, during times Tispiquin was away. He had not returned. Jacob stood on the porch and stared at Tispiquin's ivory. He so wanted to believe that Tispiquin, being Namasket's sachem and married to Philip's sister, would carry weight with Philip.

Jacob went back into the cabin, walked over to the bed, and lifted the curtain aside. Damaris was wrapped in her down cover, sound asleep with her back to him. "Lord, thank you for blessing me with such a loving, patient, kind woman," he whispered. He was about to wake her when there was a rustle from the east loft, and down the ladder came Ruth. "Good morning, Father. Are you going back upriver today? Are you going to see the Bonds?"

The girl's voice woke Damaris, who rolled over and sat on the edge of the bed by the time Ruth appeared. She smiled sleepily up at them. "You could check in on Thomas's mother, and see how she is doing. The time is coming when they will need someone to come and help care for her." She reached out and drew Ruth to her on the side of the bed. "Ruth could go. Look at her. She's become a young woman."

Damaris's glance caught Jacobs's knowing eye. "There might be something useful she could learn to do that would be of help to them in caring for Thomas's mother."

Damaris smiled. "Staying with the Bonds could provide an opportunity for her to spend some time away from the confines of the praying town, and learn more about colonial life." She stood up. "Mary will not be needing her sister's help now that Betty Sassamon is there to help with her children."

Ruth dropped her head down on her mother's shoulder. "If I were given the choice," she lifted her head and shifted to where she was eye to eye with her mother, "I'd choose Massachusetts Bay."

Jacob saw in the faces of the two women that the issue was settled. "I will tie the Bond visit in with my survey work upriver. The sooner, the better," he stated, then went on his way to the west of the cabin and stood beneath the loft. "Francis, wake up." Jacob aimed his voice toward the opening. "We need to go back to our responsibilities upriver."

The thought of doing his normal work lifted his spirits. "We will stop by Tinkham's on our way."

In the livery, they loaded the wagon. Jacob carefully attached linen paper to the drawing board along with the alidade. "We are very close to beginning mapping."

Francis packed the 33-foot chain, marking pins, felling ax, and a hatchet. Then he patted the sheath that held a knife he used to mark the witness trees. He chuckled. "At least we are not running rocks to mark a point on the ground." He made sure he had the tally belt to keep track of the numbers.

When Jacob was alone at the job site, he wondered what had kept Tispiquin away from home for so long. He turned to talk to the horse. "I feel that I should offer for Amie to stay with us, should her husband spend too much time away. Damaris and Amie are like sisters." He rubbed his hand over Barge's wide, flat cheek. "That would make Damaris happy. I'd feel better about leaving Damaris if she had a friend when we go to survey, more so when both women are alone and we men aren't there as protectors."

Chapter Sixteen

❧Hostility❧

Damaris

Afternoon Jacob went back to his survey work upriver, Damaris decided to move his rocker out onto the porch and watch for Tispiquin. She wondered if he would return with Wampapaquan.

There was a breeze that put an end to the stale, sultry air. The leaves began to flip around on their stems, showing their undersides. Of a sudden, they became still. The static caused Damaris to look toward the west, where a gray cloud was billowing upward.

Tispiquin appeared and, without acknowledging her, entered his cabin. She heard loud voices and commotion. The door of Amie's house flung open. Tispiquin came bursting out with his pagamigon in his belt and over-the-shoulder bandolier bag bulging. He moved quickly toward Philip's camp.

Lightning flashed. Thunder echoed and rain poured down upon the town.

Amie made her way across the suddenly muddy street, holding her hand on her forehead to protect her eyes from the heavy rain. "I didn't want him to go," she said, and put her hand on the porch post. "He thinks he can prevent Philip's retaliation."

"Retaliation?" Damaris's body tensed.

"Plymouth has decided to hold Wampapaquan prisoner." Amie found a seat closer to the cabin wall, away from the pouring rain. "They are deliberating as to what they will do with him. They will not let him out on Tispiquin's bail unless the Narragansett, Pequot, and Philip's Wampanoag move away from their threatening posture." There was a huge clap of thunder above Amie and Damaris while they sat on the porch and waited for the storm to pass in Tispiquin's wake.

Tispiquin

Tispiquin felt the torrent saturate his leather leggings, seep in through the purple and white beads he had slung over his shoulder, then roll down his back. He had to wipe his eyes in the constant rain. The thick mud his moccasins had packed on them from the road began to drop off in clumps and globs on the wooded path that led to Philip's camp. Lightning flashed and lit up the trees and sky. Seconds later there was a crack, boom, and the sound as if a rounded boulder rolled overhead. It shook the sky. Tispiquin was barely aware of the violent storm outside of himself as his personal tempest raged on. His world was imploding. His wife was upset over the sale of his Namasket lands. His daughter was still angry with him over his belief in the innocence of Tobias. One of his close friends had just been unjustly executed, and now Philip was becoming allied with his former enemies.

When the storm had passed, Tispiquin rested and looked around at his surroundings. The bark on the trees was saturated dark by the water that had made it through the canopy of dripping leaves. He expanded his chest and drew through his nostrils the musky steam that rose from the flora.

That was when he heard the drums.

Tispiquin was so overpowered by the primal stir of the rhythmic, quick beat of the war dance that his hand rummaged around in his bandolier bag until it felt the cool, smooth surface of his salt-glazed flask. He pulled the basswood plug and took an ample swig before he proceeded in the direction of the sound.

It was not long before he saw the glow of a huge fire through the trees. The silhouetted motion of dancers and the drumbeat stirred ancient tribal roots from a faraway continent. He took one more draw from his flask before he plugged it and shoved it back into his bag.

Philip and the Pequot and Narragansett sachems were in a huddle on the other side of the drummers and dancers. The night was young. He would entreat with them later. It had been far too long since he had participated in a tribal dance.

Tispiquin entered the circle and became one with the beat and the shrill of the high-pitched, cascading, repetitive vocables of the Wampanoag and Pequot warriors. Captivated in the moment, his feet rose and fell with the rhythm that was earthy, tribal, primal. He relived the days of his youth when he had been sought out by the whalers to be their harpooner. Tispiquin whooped and danced, air-spearing the whales of his past. For how long, he did not know, but then, somewhere in the midst of it all, he opened his eyes to the fact that the Pequot, Narragansett, and many of Philip's men were worked up to the point that they had knives drawn and were cutting themselves and drawing blood. The wild dance abruptly lost its coercive appeal when he realized they were serious about making war on the colonies.

This was not a gathering to express superior skill of what had been. This was a fierce demonstration of enmity to come.

Tispiquin made his way to the outer circle to speak with Philip. He hoped he was not too late. "The Governor will give us Wampapaquan if you withdraw away from here," he said.

Philip threw his shoulders back and lifted his chin. The cluster of feathers tied to his scalp lock began to spin in the wind. His eyes flashed. "They will pay for the death of Tobias and Mattashunnamo." He drew Tispiquin's attention to the other tribes in the war dance. "My father's enemy, the Pequot, are with me." His lips drew tight. He reached out and put the palm of his hand on Tispiquin's chest. "You tell Plymouth: In my land, I am King."

That night the newly allied, former enemies joined forces. Philip led the Wampanoag, Pequot, and Narragansett in the direction of Swansea where some of the English jury-men lived.

———

Tispiquin followed behind the foray. The brief escape from his reality passed, and now he was heading into the unknown. Philip's father, Massasoit, had been the one to approach the original Pilgrims of Plymouth in order to form a coalition with them against the Pequot and Narraganset. And now his son, Philip, had formed an alliance with those very tribes. Tispiquin recalled the day he had accepted the red riding coat as a gift from his wife's father for his own unique abilities. In later years, Massasoit had honored him for valor fighting against the Pequot. Yet today, Tispiquin understood the urgency Philip felt in putting a stop to the continuous influx of the English. His heart was torn between the Christian English and the others who were not. Tispiquin could not perceive any way to solve this. If only Philip could differentiate between Christian and heathen English. Then he thought, "If only Plymouth would have allowed Philip's Wampanoag to handle John Sassamon's death." Even so, the pressure to pay an annual tribute to Philip was becoming unbearable to the towns of Namasket and Middleborough.

Tispiquin's heart ached at the thought of Asowetow, who was at odds with him. She had lost her husband and blamed Philip for the death. She'd wanted the English to punish those she felt were responsible.

If only he could have been able to get Tobias to talk about what happened. He wanted to hear the truth of the matter. But now that Tobias was dead, there would be more deaths. Many more.

The sun began to rise. Tispiquin thought perhaps Philip and the others might be in the same state as when a harpooned whale would sound too deep. He remembered back in the day, after he had released a harpoon, a whale would thrash, frantic, then dive deep. The whale would hold its breath underwater for a long, long time before it would surface to blow out of its spout an explosive geyser of water and air, and once he had, the creature would settle. That is the moment Tispiquin would wait for to deliver the fatal blow.

However, the Pequot had no intention of settling. They still carried angst toward the English from the war fifty years ago. Against a tidal wave like this, Tispiquin was powerless to end the life of this hostility. Before the war party arrived at Swansea, he reached into his bandolier, drew out his flask, and drained its contents. He concealed himself behind a tree and watched the war party wait outside the Swansea church.

When the meeting came to an end, they ambushed the parishioners as they were leaving the service. The men who had served on the jury were singled out and violently put to death. The others scattered in a panic before a few men were able to regroup and get arms.

Tispiquin ran with the retreating warriors; some fell to his left and some to his right. Bullets whizzed all around.

The next day they found a safe place to rest. Philip approached Tispiquin. "It is true, what they say about you." He turned Tispiquin around and examined him for wounds and found none. "You do possess the power to reflect bullets. It is true. I have seen it for myself." He took from around his neck a unique crystal charm affixed to a thong, and placed it around Tispiquin's neck. "Perhaps your powers will rub off on me."

Tispiquin had just lifted the naturally faceted gem up to catch the light when a runner came into camp from the direction of Plymouth and interrupted. "Because of Swansea, Plymouth brought Wampapaquan out and shot him dead."

When the Pequot and Narragansett heard these words, they began to plan the next village to attack. Philip commanded, "We will waste the praying towns."

Tispiquin felt a twinge of guilt, because he did not believe that he had legendary powers to deflect bullets, yet he reached out and took hold of Philip's arm, "Amie is your sister." Philip attempted to pull himself away, but Tispiquin held firm. "You have to do something to stop them."

The gust of wind that blew through the bivouac did not disturb the staredown between the two. "You see them." Philip tilted his head in the direction of the Pequot, "They have come to my aid on their terms." His lips pursed and his stubborn stare held.

"It's my wife, your sister...." The glare in Philip's eyes made Tispiquin feel like all control was lost. "Tell them. Tell them Tispiquin says, spare my people and I will lend my supernatural warrior ability to the cause."

Tispiquin watched Philip enter into a council with the Pequot and Narragansett.

He was still waiting when night fell. Tispiquin heard the drums begin, but instead of stirring his primal instincts, he sat alone by a small fire and longed for the anesthetic effect of rum. While he waited, he relived the trial when his son-in-law's body had flopped over and bled afresh. He relived the complete mayhem in the courtroom that led to a hasty conclusion of guilt. He relived the thought of his close friend Tobias dying at the end of a rope. Tobias wouldn't have murdered John. Why hadn't Tobias explained what had happened?

Suddenly the drumming stopped. Everyone's attention was on the sky whose stars were shining brightly, while at the same time the moon began to slowly become black. The silence was eerie. Then slowly, very slowly, the moon's light began to re-appear, leaving a small sliver that was in the image of what looked to him like a bow.

When he looked toward the dance ground he could see the warriors were seeing the sign in the sky. After a brief time of hush, there came rousing war whoops. Tispiquin stood up and saw their bows, pagamigons, tomahawks, and rifles rise up. The drums resumed.

Philip returned. "They have agreed to allow your people and their colonial friends to live, but the village will be destroyed. You will be responsible for your people. Hide them in my summer hunting camp. There is enough food to keep them for a short time." Philip drew himself up as tall and straight as he could to Tispiquin, who was a much larger man, and said, "You must separate the colonials and send them to Plymouth or Massachusetts Bay where they belong. That is the agreement."

Since this was the best Tispiquin could do, he made the pledge sign to King Philip in the presence of the other tribal sachems. For Amie's safety and the lives of his friends, he would lend his support.

Chapter Seventeen

⚜The Black Squirrel⚜

Jacob

Jacob stretched the kinks out of his back after a full day of surveying. Francis and Ephraim were busy with the fire, pulling out the hard tack and dried meat for their evening meal.

A black squirrel jumped down out of a tree and dashed through their camp.

Jacob smiled, remembering Hobomoko's warning to never kill one of the rare creatures.

Jacob heard a distinctive click before the hammer of Francis's gun dropped. Francis had already sighted in on the creature.

"Francis, wait," he said, but it was too late.

Francis went over to retrieve his catch.

"Why did you try to stop me?" Francis asked before he held up the limp, headless body of the squirrel. "Fresh meat."

Jacob gave a half smile. "Probably doesn't mean much, but when I was young, Hobomoko stopped me from killing a black squirrel." He paused. "Hobomoko told me that black squirrels are sacred. They are like albinos, just something special about 'em and it's best to just leave 'em be." He reached for a green branch and made a skewer while Francis skinned and cleaned the catch. Ephraim stirred up the coals and built a spit. It wasn't much meat to go around, but it was bound to be tasty.

"Tell us about what it was like in Plymouth in the old days, when you were young," Ephraim said.

"When I was young?" Jacob felt as though he, himself had just been shot in the gut with such a question. When I was young? In spite of hurt pride, the question caused his mind to travel back in time. "Plymouth was just being built. I would watch the men march around under the command of Captain Miles Standish. Hobomoko lived with Captain Standish. The Captain would let me march around as long as I promised to stay out of the way. It seemed like they were always preparing for an attack that never came, but when they weren't doing that, I would sometimes be allowed to go beaver hunting with Hobomoko. He's the one who showed me everything I know about beaver snaring." He lifted his head to focus his eyes on his son. "It's too bad that beaver and muskrat are starting to become so scarce, but back in those days, we could lay out a trap line and bring in a harvest the very next day. Have I told you about fish in the river? The herring, back then in Namasket, we could walk across the river on the backs of the running herring."

Jacob talked about the old days so long that the moon was full and bright by the time the three realized how much time had passed.

Then, without any hint or warning, the moonlight began to fade. Jacob stopped talking and focused on the eerie event in the night sky. Shadows fell across the camp and the moon disappeared before their eyes. Then, just as it had gone to black, it began to return a little at a time. The hairs on the back of Jacob's neck stood up when a strange sign that looked like a bow appeared. Jacob remembered that Hobomoko told him once that a solar eclipse happened because the black squirrel ate the sun.

He stopped himself from thinking or saying anything about the omen, and instead told Ephraim, "Tomorrow, I'm leaving the finishing touches of the mapping to you." He turned to Francis. "I am trusting you to finish up everything else here while I check in on Damaris's relatives." Jacob cleared his throat. "When you two finish up, which shouldn't take all day, I want you to come and meet me up there."

Jacob went on his way, dodging horses, wagons, and dressed-up pedestrians. This was where the wealthy people lived. Not everyone was wealthy, though. He also passed clusters of working people talking together. Then he passed militiamen and heard one of them say under his breath, "What is that? An Englishman or an Indian?" Jacob kept on walking until he arrived at the inn. The place was grand in comparison to the humble homes Jacob had known all of his life. To the left of the entryway was the tavern. It was quiet, with the exception of the maid, who was busy cleaning and preparing the room for the day's patrons. A smell lingered in the air that reminded Jacob of Damaris's father's establishment in Plymouth. Jacob breathed in the essence of stale smoke and spilled beer and remembered. Was this really the best place for Ruth?

His thoughts were interrupted by Thomas Bond.

"Jacob. Good to see you." Thomas looked past Jacob. "Where is your lovely wife, Damaris, and your daughter Ruth?"

Sara Bond walked into the great hall from the other side. "Welcome, Jacob. Is Damaris not well? She didn't come with you?"

"Damaris is well. She asked me to come, since I was surveying nearby, and see how your mother's health is doing. She wanted me to find out if you need our help." He paused. "There has been a great deal happening in our town and in Plymouth. Damaris was hoping to come for a visit and hoped that Ruth could help with your mother. Damaris would like to visit and be here to help Ruth learn her duties."

Sara motioned in the direction of the room she had come from. "Come, let me take you in to see Mother."

Jacob followed the Bonds through the living quarters into a room off the parlor.

Sara opened the door. "Mother, we have company. Jacob Cooke. Damaris Hopkins's husband." She took hold of Jacob's wrist and led him to face the old woman. "It's Jacob. He's here on business and stopped by."

It was a bright, cheerful, stinky room. Everything was neat and tidy. Warm light shone through the window, but the room smelled as though the chamber pot had not been dumped in a week. "Hello, Mrs. Bond. Damaris has been asking about you," Jacob said to the frail, bent-over frame of an ancient woman with her chin on her chest.

The old lady lifted her head and focused. He watched her cloudy blue eyes brighten and saw the corners of her droopy mouth lift. "Damaris. Dear, sweet girl, Damaris. Did I hear you say she was coming to see me?"

"Yes, and she is bringing our daughter Ruth with her," he explained. Jacob wondered how Damaris and Ruth were going to be able to do this work. He was more than happy to survey and was thankful that his work was in God's great outdoors where he could enjoy the fresh air.

Thinking about surveying reminded him of Francis and Ephraim. He said to Thomas, "I would like to requisition dinner for three for tonight. My son and neighbor have done well learning, and I want to give them a good meal."

"Very well. I will let the cook know. We are cooking a roast beef dinner with carrots and cabbage."

"Sounds good to me," came a weak voice. "God bless."

"God bless you too, Mrs. Bond," Jacob said before leaving her room.

Jacob arrived back at the inn from his errands and sat on the grand porch only a short time before Francis and Ephraim appeared from the direction of the livery.

Ephraim stepped up toward Jacob. "I have a few details to add to the map when we get back." He held his hand out toward Jacob. "It won't take long for me to do it."

He was followed by Francis. "Something smells good in there. What are we having?"

"They cooked roast beef with carrots and cabbage." Jacob led the way through the swinging door into the tavern where their table was already set and waiting. The room was filled with the smell of the roast beef mixed with fresh tobacco smoke coming from clay pipes. This smelled much better than the stale air he had encountered earlier in the day. Men from all walks of life were gathered in clusters, discussing the day.

Mrs. Sara Bond herself brought the meal to them. "Would anyone like a tankard of ale?"

"Very much." Francis's teeth became visible. "They will as well," he added, motioning toward his father and Ephraim.

After the meal, Jacob left Francis and Ephraim at the table with their ale and went outside on the porch. Below the porch, several of the local militia were armed and standing around talking with Thomas. "You say, they were all fired up?" Thomas's eyes were wide and the color drained from his face when he spoke.

"Yes," one of the men said.

"Those heathen savages attacked Swansea and killed people as they were coming out of a church service," said another soldier.

The back of Jacob's neck warmed. "Swansea?" he asked.

"Governor Leverett said that starting a war is wicked and without cause. It is down right barbarous what they have done." The tall one waved his hand in the direction of the Governor's office. "Leverett has put out the word for us to call out the militia to go down and assist Plymouth."

The heavy-set soldier nodded his head in agreement. "Governor Winslow is quite concerned that the attack came from Pequot."

Pequot. Jacob didn't wait to hear any more. He turned around and went inside to get Francis and Ephraim. He took the tankard of ale from Francis's hand and set it firmly on the table. "We have to go. I've got some very grave news."

Chapter Eighteen

Broken

Excerpt from the writings of Damaris Cooke,
1677 Massachusetts.

Amie and I cooked and ate one meal together
every day while our husbands were away. Jacob
and I planned for his return to be in time for the
flax harvest. Tispiquin should have been back at
Namasket days earlier, and Amie was concerned. I
remember that I did my best to comfort and assure
her, but even Sassamon didn't leave Betty for this
long without sending word.

In the past, when our men went to hunting or
on a survey, Amie and I would think it a welcome
time to take on community tasks we would not
ordinarily be free to do, but this just felt different,
and I honestly didn't like it.

Damaris

In the early morning light, Damaris stood in the road, brought Ruth's head tight against her chest, and watched her home as it was consumed in flames. She was surrounded by the sound of roar and crackle. The whole town was ablaze.

Warriors shrieked and flashed past, their red-painted and oiled bodies reflecting the flames. She was sure the earth beneath her feet was shaking as much as Ruth. The din and chaos going on was so horrific that she moved her hand to cover Ruth's eyes. She stood frozen in the heat. Her friends and neighbors hurried to escape their burning homes. Through the surrounding smoke, in the distance, Middleborough was under attack as well.

Mary Sipit's desperate voice called, "Sara!" Having found the girl, Mary ran past with her shrieking grandchild in her arms. They left a swirl of smoke in their wake.

Clamorous screams and the shrill of war whoops echoed through the remains of the town. Then, as suddenly as they had come, the bellows of the warriors grew faint. King Philip's allies disappeared into the woods. Damaris continued to gaze in glaciated silence. She could not get her body to move except to rock back and forth, holding tightly to her young daughter.

Through the sparks, smoke, and floating debris, a strong voice ordered from horseback, "Everybody, gather in the cow commons."

Damaris realized the voice was Francis's, and she loosened her grip on Ruth. Francis was back. If Francis was here, perhaps Jacob was close by. She rubbed her eyes to squint and was able to see Francis ride through the smoke and up the incline.

"Everybody, gather in the cow commons," he repeated.

Damaris followed along with the others. "We are going to be alright," she assured Ruth.

The cattle had escaped from the pasture and were roaming about helter-skelter. Damaris continued to move among the bleating sheep and goats. She and Ruth had to step over a dead ewe and through feculent matter, dry and wet.

Amie grabbed hold of Damaris's arm. "There you are!"

Damaris felt a flush of joy in the midst of the chaos when she hugged her friend, squeezing the girl between them.

Amie's eyes were wide. She pointed toward a fallen goat. "Our animals--so many are dead." Her trembling voice sounded above the din. "What is going to happen to us?"

Damaris, Ruth, and Amie sat together. Damaris watched Mary's husband, Joseph, emerge from the smoke with Wannoo and join another huddle in the cow commons. Families were reuniting under the protection of the town's makeshift militia. She waited and worried they would be attacked again.

Damaris noticed Amie's eyes were red from more than the smoke as they stared at each other. Tears began to flow.

The smoke hung in the air while they sat in their huddle among all the others and watched their cabins, barns, and a year's communal hard work be consumed.

Amie assisted Mary Sipit in comforting her granddaughter.

Damaris didn't move or cry when Ruth left her side to join Amie, consoling little Sara.

Damaris watched Ruth pat the child's head. "We will be okay." Ruth's voice was reassuring to the child, but Damaris herself sat silently terrified. As time passed, she remained uncommunicative, until she heard Jacob's voice.

"Damaris, Damaris? Where are you? Damaris?"

She pushed herself up from the ground and saw Barge first, then the rider. "Jacob, Jacob! Over here!" She waved. "We are over here."

Jacob dismounted and took his wife and daughter into his arms. "Thank God you are okay." He raised his hand and pointed beyond the commons. "Betty's cabin still stands. It was too far from here to bother with."

"Where's Francis?" Damaris asked. "I saw him earlier."

"He's fine. He went to Middleborough to help there." He put his hands on Damaris's shoulders. "I'm taking you women to Betty's cabin and I want you to stay put until I can come up with a plan." His voice was firm and commanding. "You must keep Amie away from any militia man you do not recognize. Do you understand?"

Damaris stared back at her husband blankly.

Jacob's face tightened. "The men are blind with rage against the Indians. If they knew she was King Philip's sister," he paused, "I just don't know what they might do to her." His face relaxed a little. He breathed in. "Some of the volunteers from the frontier towns are out to do harm to any Indian they see and don't care if they are from a praying town or not." He took hold of the reigns in one hand and his wife's hand in the other. Ruth and Amie followed.

Damaris looked back to them. "Come, we will have some protection over there."

Amie

Later, in the cabin, Amie could hear the beat of her heart pound in her ears. She opened Betty's curtains, then quickly closed them before she settled down on the fur-covered bench and placed her arm around Ruth. "Everything will be alright. Tispiquin went to put a stop to the Pequot and Narragansett. I am praying to God that he will convince my brother to calm them down." Amie felt the trembling of Ruth's body and brought the girl's head into her shoulder. With her hand, she stroked her tousled hair.

Ruth turned her head and looked up. "What is going to happen to us?"

"Once Tispiquin is able to get things to calm down, we will rebuild here at Betty's Neck." She gently leaned Ruth back toward her mother, stood up, and walked over to the door.

Amie stood on the threshold and took inventory of the situation outside in the cow commons. The smoke was lifting. Groups of people sat in clusters waiting for direction. The local militia were standing guard. They were waiting, too. She felt a pulse of relief when she realized that the villagers were all there. Joy arose in her heart. She counted them. There were no strangers. "They are all here. Not one was killed in the raid."

People would be hungry. She looked toward Damaris. "We need to build a fire and cook something so we can feed everybody." She stepped back into the cabin, happy that she had a newfound purpose. "Damaris, Ruth, go back to the larder and see what you can find. I'll start the fire."

———

Amie was bent down with a small wooden cup of broth for Wannoo and almost dropped it when she heard the sound of Tispiquin's voice, "Wampanoag, prepare to follow me."

Amie barely had a chance to give the cup to Wannoo when Tispiquin took her up to give her a directive. "I want the men with me. You gather the women and children and follow us. I have plans for a camp."

Amie looked back at her colonial friends who were in a fearful huddle. She took Damaris's hand and put her arm around Ruth. "But what about our friends?"

"Colonials must take refuge in one of the colonies or die." His hand firmly guided Amie in the direction he expected her to go. "Han yo."

Then Tispiquin spoke with authority to Ephraim Tinkham. "Get your people out now or they will die. You will be out of harm's way in Massachusetts Bay or Plymouth. You must make haste. I have made arrangement for this."

Chapter Nineteen

❧Going Their Separate Ways❧

Excerpt from the writings of Damaris Cooke,
1677 Massachusetts.

   I wish Tispiquin could have persuaded Philip
not to do violence. I have seen Philip angry and
it did not sit well with me. I think back to when
Amie and I were little. We were playing in the
woods and we saw Philip become angry with one
of the camp dogs. Amie and I saw him beat the poor
thing for not dropping a dead duck when he asked
him to. As long as I had known him, Philip had
been strong-willed and prideful.

   The magistrates in Massachusetts Bay and
Plymouth took John Eliot's advice and decided that
it would be in the best interests of the clean-handed
Christian Indians of the praying towns to be protected from Philip's marauders and enraged settlers.
They set aside Deer Island near Massachusetts Bay
as a safe haven.

   Betty had already chosen to settle in with Mary,
which worked out well for them both. I was thankful to God that Mary's heart had been changed.

   There was a deep sadness in my heart when I
watched Tispiquin lead his people away, because I
had no way of knowing where he was taking them.

   The Tinkhams decided that they would go back
to Plymouth. Jacob brought Ruth and me to Mas-

sachusetts Bay, where we stayed at the Inn with the Bonds.

I promised Amie that I would always be her friend and help her in any way I could. She prom-ised me the same.

Damaris

Damaris watched Tispiquin lead his small band down the trail into the woods and wondered where he might take them. The last person to leave was Amie, who lingered behind, making sure all the Wampanoag were safely following his lead. Damaris reached out and took Amie's hand. "May all of you stay safe until we meet again."

Amie's arms encircled Ruth and Damaris before she said, "If I get to the Bay Colony, I will look for you."

Damaris held tight to Amie's waist and heard her say, "I pray this turmoil ends soon and we can come back here and rebuild."

The party following Tispiquin was almost out of sight when she gave Amie one last hug before she withdrew. "I do, too."

"I do too," Damaris said again and again, while she and Ruth held each other tight and watched Amie disappear into the woods. They stood arm in arm for a long time before they walked back to the Sassamon cabin.

Damaris and Ruth had no sooner said farewell to Amie than they went through another sad separation. Ephraim Tinkham gathered his family and the others who were going to Plymouth.

Not one of the remaining small group was a preacher or church leader, but they felt the need to pray, so they gathered into a small circle. Finally, Ephraim broke out in singing Psalm 5. Everyone joined.

Give ear to my words, O Lord, consider my meditation.

Hearken unto the voice of my cry, my King, and my God: for unto thee will I pray.

My voice shalt thou hear in the morning, O Lord; in the morning will I direct my prayer unto thee, and will look up.

Damaris and Ruth were now the only family left in Namasket, so they went back into the cabin. Ruth dipped out another bowl of the pottage for her mother and herself and settled down by the small fire. "At least we won't go hungry, as long as we stay here."

Damaris noticed that Ruth's skirt and overblouse were quite worn and looked shabby. "You poor, dear girl, I had intended to work on new clothes for you as soon as the harvest work was done. We had only to prepare the flax and wool for the weaving. Your father and brother tanned several hides and had them ready." Damaris sighed and ran her hand over the soft surface of her own skirt. "Only yesterday I finished this. And to think, only yesterday, I had yours cut and ready for assembly, when..." Tears filled her eyes. "When—when all this happened." She looked intently at her daughter through tears. "I do pray your father comes for us soon."

"I do, too," Ruth said and wriggled close to her mother on the fur bench. "Father, please come soon," she whispered, and put her head on Damaris's shoulder. The quietness screamed around them when Ruth whispered, "Mother, I'm afraid."

Amie

Amie's calves and upper thighs burned from the hard pace. She found it difficult trying to keep up with Tispiquin. He led them on a trail that would have become overgrown if it had not been for the use it received from the deer, bear, porcupine, and other forest creatures. Wampanoag lands were like that. And there was good reason for letting land go feral. If a hunting ground had been heavily used, it would be left alone for many years so that when they came back to it, it would be replenished with wildlife.

Wannoo had trouble keeping pace with the men and was now with Joseph Sipit and the women. Even though they lagged behind, Amie and Mary Sipit set a pace that was doable with children and elders.

Wannoo took charge of Amie's slower-moving pack. "I will read sign, track Tispiquin."

After they had gone a considerable distance, Wannoo came to a fork in the path and began to examine the trails for signs. Amie sat on a fallen log. Mary Sipit joined her there. "Do you know where we are going?"

"Inland toward the west, as far as I can tell." Amie stood up and looked for the position of the sun. "We have been going in a southwest direction."

Wannoo walked back and forth, inspecting leaves and twigs. "This way." He pointed out a bent sapling that was leaning southwest.

Amie's body continued to complain as she trudged along behind Wannoo. "This late in the day, I'm not looking forward to the work it will take for us to make camp."

Wannoo paused in the trail, lifted his head, pointed his nose in the air and sniffed. "We are getting close, I smell campfire."

When the women and children finally arrived in the clearing and saw the small fires, Amie reached her hand out to their guide. "Thank you, Wannoo."

Amie walked over to where Tispiquin and the men were about finished making a camp out of the bark and supplies that had been stored by her brother's people when they left.

Amie could see that Tispiquin stood with his arms crossed and that he was staring. He looked like he had something weighty on his mind when she approached him. "I don't know what you said to my brother, but whatever it was saved our lives."

Tispiquin glanced about the camp that he and the men had just built.

Amie's eyes brightened when she realized what the men had accomplished. "I see the lodges are all ready for us."

Even though Tispiquin continued to struggle with the tempest, he gently touched her hair. "Make food."

Amie and the women set to digging up pottery vessels. They found the cache that held kernels of corn. They were glad there was enough in the stores for them to prepare pottage.

After everyone had settled, Amie took a short walk by herself. She stopped to lean against a tree. She breathed the evening air into her lungs, let it out slowly, and whispered to her Creator, "I don't know what the future will be." She paused and absorbed His Creation, the beauty of the orange and yellow setting sun as it glowed through the silhouette of the trees.

Amie inventoried her surroundings and thought about where Damaris would be sleeping this night. "Lord, I pray Damaris and her family will find a safe place to live at the Bay

Colony. Thank you, Lord Jesus, that our Namasket people's lives are spared."

She smiled. "It was Tispiquin. Somehow he convinced the warriors to spare them all.

"I can tell by the way Tispiquin is behaving, the price was immense."

Chapter Twenty

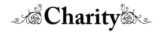 **Charity**

Excerpt from the writings of Damaris Cooke, 1677 Massachusetts.

From the day Jacob delivered us safely to the Bonds, there was never a dull moment. Thomas Bond's mother and Ruth took to each other right off in spite of the age difference between the two. Ruth and Momma Bond would talk for hours, whispering and giggling. I thanked the Lord for these long conversations, as they seemed healing for both of them.

Perhaps because Momma Bond had lived through the Pequot war, she could relate to Ruth's recent trauma. And Ruth's very presence brightened the sickroom.

Sometimes, when the old lady didn't think her daughter-in-law or I were near enough to hear, she would prompt Ruth to sing an Algonquin chant. And then she would say, "Oh, my dear, your little song was lovely. Now tell me again, where did you learn the song?"

Ruth would tell her once again that she had learned it from Asowetow. I would hear the frail

voice beg, "Won't you make an old lady happy and
sing to me again?"

I, on the other hand, did not much want to
sit and talk about what we had been through. I
kept my feelings to myself with the exception of my
prayers. I told a great deal to the Lord and nobody
else.

Damaris

The time had come when Damaris had to let the fires go completely out in order to clean the accumulation of soot. This caused the dining room to be exceptionally chilly. Damaris was on her hands and knees and had her head in the hearth, her small, flat shovel in hand, and her bucket by her side when she heard the familiar voice of a dear old friend. She rose up so quickly at the sound of his voice that she upset her ash bucket, causing a poof of gray that was like the smoke of a puffball in the heat of summer. "John Eliot!" she squealed and ran and threw her arms around him. "Have you seen Amie? How are my friends from Namasket? What do you know?" When she stepped back she saw the imprint of ash on his black clothing and realized that she was covered in a layer of ash from her dust cap to her white chemise and apron. She tried to wipe and brush herself, but the ash clung to her. "Oh, dear. I'm so sorry. Truly I am."

John brushed the dust from his jacket and chuckled. "Damaris. What a delightful surprise! I never expected to find you in Massachusetts Bay."

Damaris let all the things that she had pent up since the attack on the praying town pour out to her friend.

John Eliot raised two fingers and gently placed them on her mouth. "I truly want to hear, but I'm late for a meeting at the church."

She saw in his eyes that he was sincere, and went mute.

"I stopped in here this morning to put in a requisition for tonight's dinner. Make sure you mark me down. I will be able to talk at length then."

He opened the door and looked back. "Damaris, I do have news about Amie, but I need more time than this."

Damaris's excitement fell flat, yet she stepped outside to watch John disappear in the direction of the white church. A chickadee landed on the arm of the chair nearby and made a little chirp. "He will be back," she told the bird, and went back inside.

Later that evening, the dining room had a fresh, new fire aglow, and the room was warm and as cozy as a room that large could be with candlelight, hot stew, ale, and conversation.

Damaris had purposefully set the three-legged table over to the right of the hearth, opposite the wood box. She had set a place for her friend and two chairs, even though she would not be eating her dinner with him. Instead she had planned to accompany him by taking tea while he ate.

She busied herself serving and clearing tables until John Eliot finally came in. He was not alone like he had said he would be, but when she saw that he was with Jacob she almost dropped her pitcher and rag. Instead, she set them down on the three-legged table and ran to greet Jacob and John.

"I know he didn't requisition a meal," John said. "I insist Jacob let me share mine with him."

Jacob enveloped his wife. "Damaris, I didn't expect to be able to get back so soon, but our men are heading out to the Connecticut valley in the morning, and my lieutenant has given me leave so that I can say goodbye to you." Then he stepped back and smiled toward John. "And then on my way here, look who I ran into!"

Damaris quickly found an extra chair to squeeze into the small area. "We will have to make the best of it," she said, and shifted the table before she left to get the stew.

When she came back, the two were so deep into their conversation she felt like a little girl holding a stick, wanting to participate in a game of hoop and stick while the others were leaving her out. Not in a way that they wanted to be mean or anything, just so into what they were doing it seemed like they had forgotten she was even there. Nonetheless, she was able to wriggle her chair in to where she could hear what they were talking about.

Jacob leaned toward John Eliot's ear. "What I heard was that Captain Church and his men rode into Tispiquin's camp and rounded everybody up and took them to Deer Island to be put under guard."

John Eliot's eyes looked toward Damaris. "I don't mean to be rude, but I should very much like more tea."

Jacob cleared his throat. "And I could sure use an ale." He flashed a glance back to the preacher and back to Damaris before she had a chance to say a word. Jacob said, "The Bible tells us not to get drunk and act like a fool. I don't intend to get drunk or act like a fool." He smiled.

Damaris didn't argue. She took their bowls and went to pour them each their requested beverage.

"Hey, wench! Bring me more ale," a gruff voice hollered in Damaris's direction from the middle of the room.

She saw the pain in Jacob's face when she forced a smile. "Yes sir, right away." She quickly gave the man the ale she held in her hand and scurried back to get more for Jacob and the tea for John. She did not want to miss out on what they were talking about. She gave them each their drink and sat down to listen.

"I was told," Jacob said, "Captain Church left two elders at the camp with plenty of food and left a message for Tispiquin that if he wants his wife back, he should meet Church at Plymouth because he had an important mission in mind for him."

Reverend Eliot took a small sip of tea. "It is a sin for Captain Church to be believing in all that superstition that Tispiquin has supernatural warrior powers." He took another sip and stared at Jacob. "Not only that, it wasn't right to take God's people hostage."

Jacob nodded. "But at least they were taken to Deer Island. You helped to set that island aside as a safe place for the people from your praying towns."

"Yes, I know, but things are not going as well as I had hoped." John sighed. "It is becoming more and more difficult to gather enough supplies to feed and clothe them, and winter is setting in early." He finally looked directly at Damaris. "I owe a great deal of gratitude to your daughter Mary and Amie's daughter Betty for all the work they are doing through the church in Plymouth to help gather provision." His eyes went from Damaris to Jacob and back. "You both should be proud of Mary." Damaris felt a warm satisfaction. Her girl had learned what she had so desperately tried to teach her after all.

John took a small sip from his tea. He looked like he had something important to say.

The loud man at the center table banged his empty tankard on the table and hollered, "Wench!"

Damaris jumped up and rushed over to get the empty tankard. Mehitabel, the other woman who worked at the inn, tapped her arm and nodded her head toward Jacob. "I got this, Damaris dear, you go back and enjoy your husband."

Excerpt from the writings of Damaris Cooke, 1677 Massachusetts.

After Mehitabel relieved me from my duties in the dining room, I came back to the table and sat as close to Jacob as I could. The Bonds were nice people, and my duties there were fairly light compared to the hard labor in a praying town. In spite of the hard work, there was a satisfaction in the community we had built. I missed the old life so. I missed my simple little home, our fields of flax, and the gardens with the corn, beans, and squash. I missed the barn where we kept our animals when they were not in the cow commons. I missed my dear friend Amie.

Damaris

John Eliot stood to leave as Damaris returned. "I have put in a very hard day, but tomorrow morning I want to speak with both of you about something. Something we discussed at the church today is pressing on my mind, but I would rather wait till the morning. I want to pray about it before we speak."

The next morning, the three joined together at a more comfortable table. Damaris brought them hot sassafras tea to enjoy with breakfast.

John Eliot finally said, "It grieves my heart the way the natives that Jesus loves are being treated. I'm doing my best to bring in supplies to their only safe place, but my main concern is that I have been told your close friend, Amie, is in danger. The sinful hatred toward her brother is escalating to the point that I fear they will come seeking her out for imprisonment. Worse yet, she may be sold into slavery. It has already happened to some before they had a chance to be taken to Deer Island."

Damaris felt deep grief and guilt that she was safe and her friend was in danger. "Is there anything I can do? Where is this Deer Island?"

John Eliot leaned back and his eyes opened wide. "Damaris, I thought you knew. Deer Island is in the harbor in the bay here."

Damaris set her tea down and stood up. "You mean Amie is here in the Massachusetts Bay and I didn't know it?" She sat back down. "I shall go see her straight away."

John Eliot sucked his top lip between his teeth and held it there while he formulated his thought. "It's not all that simple." He paused and looked at Jacob. "I know this is a strange request, but if you are willing to allow Damaris to assist me in my effort to escort Amie off the island, it could very well save Amie's life."

After John Eliot laid out his tentative plan, he said, "Talk about it."

He paused and then continued. "There could be risk."

Chapter Twenty-One

⚜Deer Island, Winter 1675⚜

Excerpt from the writings of Damaris Cooke,
1677 Massachusetts.

Jacob and I talked long during the midnight
hours about Amie and what John Eliot was allud-
ing to. I was able to tell Jacob that I would rather
live in primitive conditions with my Namasket
friends on Deer Island than to be barked at by the
rumbustious men in the dining room.

There was not much time for him to talk with
John Eliot and say good-bye to Ruth and me, but
before he left he had a talk with the Bonds. I heard
him thank them for all they were doing on our
behalf, and then I heard him ask them to promise
that they would not, under any circumstance, allow
Ruth to work in the dining room and tell them that
I would be gone for an unknown length of time on
a war mission to help Reverend John Eliot.

Damaris

The wind was kicking up outside the small elm bark
dome where Damaris stretched on the lumpy ground,
wrapped in a woolen bedroll. "Do you have an old rag
in here I can use?"

Amie rolled over. "Damaris, why are you awake?"

Damaris sat up, took the poking stick, and began to single out a rock from the fire pit. "I need something to wrap a hot rock in because my feet are cold."

"Is that the only reason you can't sleep?"

"Not really. I can't get my mind off Ruth. I don't understand. Why am I worried? I know she is doing very well with the Bonds. They are good people."

Damaris noticed through the glow of the small fire that Amie's bronze countenance had changed from flawless and smooth, to a rimpled appearance about her eyes and mouth. Amie had lost weight since they parted. She and Amie had both lost their youth somewhere in their long years of friendship. She remained quiet and watched the reflection of the small flame flicker and dance in Amie's eyes.

Before long, Amie's face changed. Her mouth pulled tight and her eyebrows came together. "Oh, Damaris," Amie sighed. "My poor Tispiquin struggled much in his heart and mind before he finally made the decision to go over to Philip's camp. At first he went to try and convince him to call back the warriors, but then he could see that Philip had too many from the Pequot and Narragansett. They were fired up. Tispiquin told me that he was powerless to stop them."

"Do you think that Tispiquin will be able to come back to us, now that Captain Church went to all that trouble to bring you and the others here?"

"I know my brother. He will not trust my husband. He will not let him come back to us. Captain Church has me under guard. Tispiquin will want to rescue me." Amie raised herself up, leaning all her weight on her elbow so that she could look at Damaris across the glowing embers. "I fear that I will not see my Tispiquin again."

The concern Damaris saw in Amie's eyes mirrored her own heart. "Jacob and Francis just headed out with the militia to the Connecticut valley."

Amie shook her head and looked away.

Amie's eyes were shining in the reflected firelight. She wanted to comfort her, but all she could blurt was, "Who would have thought our good husbands could be fighting on opposing sides?"

Amie's shoulders shook and quiet tears fell. She shifted her position. "It was not my decision to be here." Her eyes closed. "I would rather be in the hunting camp or in Plymouth with Betty and Mary."

Damaris's forehead crinkled. "What is it you are trying to say?"

Amie turned her head and blinked her eyes before her words came with fear and calculation. "Tispiquin was concerned about what the English might do to me if they ever found out that I am his wife and King Philip's sister." She let out a deep sigh, "I'm caught in the middle." She became silent.

Damaris was uncomfortable with the sudden quiet and scooted a little closer to Amie. "We have never had to deal with anything like this before. We were young the last time there was any fighting in the colony. I have been eavesdropping on old Mother Bond telling Ruth about the Pequot war, and how she took in many children whose parents had died. One was named John. He was from the Massachusetts."

Amie's eyes shone in the firelight. "I don't remember much, only that your father helped my father fight the Pequot. I don't know what is going to happen. All I know is Captain Church has put me here to draw out my husband."

Damaris cleared her throat, "On John Eliot's last visit, when he brought me, he encouraged us to wait for his instructions."

Damaris could see that Amie's eyes were fearful.

"Maybe you should not have come here," Amie said.

Damaris's chest ached. "We have to wait for John Eliot, and I promised that I would be with you. You are not alone, Amie."

Amie closed and opened her eyes once more and shifted her body. "Tispiquin told me about the attack on Swansea." The whites of Amie's eyes reflected in the firelight. Her voice tensed. "Pequot warriors were so fired up that they drew blood with knives at the war dance." Amie shuddered. "Tispiquin was there."

Damaris felt the inside of her stomach tighten while Amie told about the Pequot. "Hasn't there been enough bloodshed? Attacking Swansea and burning our town should have been more than enough revenge for your brother to satisfy his anger over the executions."

Amie sighed. "I cannot understand why Plymouth did not let Tobias's son Wampapaquan go when the rope broke."

Damaris's tummy churned at the thought of the hanging. "I believe they should have let him go."

Amie sat up, reached over to the small woodpile, and gently placed another stick on the coals. "Poor Wampapaquan confessed that the other two had committed the murder just like Patuckson testified."

"Jacob agrees that they should have let Wampapaquan go." Then Damaris thought for a moment, her forehead scrunched and her eyes widened. "They might not have shot Wampapaquan if Philip had not attacked Swansea a week after the executions."

"I hate that my brother has turned against those of us who are Christians and now Plymouth and Boston Colony have raised militias to fight against him. What chance is there for the Wampanoag?"

Damaris shivered. "It is pure evil the way everybody is allowing anger and fear to take control." Damaris shifted herself, trying to find a comfortable spot. "The whole world seems to be heading straight for hell on earth."

"Why can't they see that the world would be a better place if everyone could learn to live in little towns like we had?" Amie's eyes focused on Damaris. Her face softened a bit. "I feel safer now that we are back together."

Damaris awoke to the sun's rays streaming through every little hole and crack of the elm bark dome. "Amie, wake up. We need to look for some straw to insulate this lodge." She gently placed her hand on her friend's shoulder and shook. "My feet were so cold last night, I could hardly stand it."

Damaris and Amie scouted around in over a foot of snow and found a great stand of marsh grass. They spent the better part of the day digging down through the snow to cut it off at the base. Then they hauled and stacked the long, dry reeds to help insulate the makeshift lodge.

Many in camp were gathering the marsh grass. Some were making repairs to the bark on the exterior of their wigwam, and still others were hunting for some meat to add to the community pot. Damaris let go of her armload of reeds. "I am hopeful that there will be something good in the pottage today."

"Me too," Amie said. She dropped her bundle on top. "I was beginning to wonder if this dry grass might be edible."

Damaris heard the sound of voices nearby and tapped Amie's shoulder. "I just heard someone say that the tide might be going out far enough for us to be able to dig for clams and seek out eels. I'd love to sink my teeth into some roasted eel."

"So would I. Fresh seafood will go well with boiled maize," Amie said. She pointed to the clay pots and braided corn that were hanging on a rack above the vessels. "We are fortunate that we still have a small amount of dried corn to ration now that the snow has gotten too deep to dig for ground nuts."

Damaris noticed that off in the distance, the sky had changed to golden yellow along the horizon. "This will be my last bundle," she said as she gathered up her pile of grass and looked over toward the western gate where a Militiaman stood guard. "He looks to be a boy about my son Francis's age."

Amie dropped her last bundle and nudged Damaris. "Do you see that woman talking to the guard? I wonder what she's talking to him about?"

Damaris directed her attention to the East gate, then back to Amie. "She came from where the Naticks are camped. I wonder what the sentinel and that Natick woman are talking about so intently?"

Amie straightened herself back up. "I will find out."

As soon as Amie saw the woman a safe distance from the guard, she left Damaris and went to talk with the Natick woman as she made her way toward her part of camp.

Amie came back. "The soldier told her that John Eliot is expected to come in with some needed supplies."

Damaris gazed beyond the gate. "The war is so bad out there."

Amie came along side. "She said John is late. Nobody knows if John might have been killed while trying to get through. The guards have been expecting him for two weeks now."

Damaris took hold of Amie's hand.

"Gathering donations from the Colonies and finding volunteers to help him deliver to us puts John in much danger," Amie said.

"John Eliot told me that Betty and Mary are very active in the effort. You can be proud of your daughter," Damaris told Amie on their way to join Mary Sipit and her granddaughter.

"Word is John Eliot has been delayed," Amie told the others.

"We should pray," Mary said.

The three women stood arm in arm, heads bowed. Little Sara hid herself in the folds of her grandmother's coat while they called upon the Lord to bring John Eliot and the much-needed provisions.

Chapter Twenty-Two

Loss

Damaris

Damaris was looking for firewood when she heard the camp caller bark, "John Eliot, John Eliot. Supplies, supplies." She witnessed people, some she had never seen before, scramble out of their wigwams. She dropped her piece of wood. Others dropped whatever they had been doing and hurried to welcome the preacher. She ran along with Amie. "I don't know what I'm more hungry for, the supplies or to find out the latest news." She began to slow down. "I hope there is some word about Jacob and Francis."

John Eliot brought with him a report of the latest war casualties and deaths of the men from praying towns and the volunteers from Deer Island. When he posted the list to a tree, people took turns having a chance to see whose names were on the list. When Damaris's turn came to look she found the towns of Namasket and Middleborough. She ran her finger down the linen paper past the A's and B's. She continued down to where she read the name Jacob Cooke in the C's under the column that listed the dead in the Connecticut valley. A pain like a sharp blade of an arrow forcefully shot through her heart and caused her legs to give way.

Excerpt from the writings of Damaris Cooke, 1677 Massachusetts.

I don't know how long I lay in the snow before John Eliot himself knelt down and placed his hand upon my shoulder. The kind old preacher did not say a word. He just placed his hand on my shoulder and stood by. His gentle touch opened the tide gate of my soul. My tears flowed freely, melting snow. I had no concept of the time or that the outside temperature was freezing cold.

Nearby I heard jubilation. The others unloaded the supply wagons. From what I could make of their muted voices, there must have been some good food and blankets.

I was so upset that I even asked Amie to leave me alone for a while. I did not want to go on living without Jacob, but when I came to my senses, my thoughts went to Ruth.

Jacob had been in the militia. There was a war going on. Knowing that did not help much when Damaris tried to wrap her mind around the fact that Jacob was gone. It was the never coming back; never hearing his voice; never seeing, smelling, or touching her man again kind of gone. Yet, she willed herself to say, "The Lord giveth and the Lord taketh away; blessed be the name of the Lord." Her weak legs wobbled when she rose up with John Eliot's help. He couldn't stay; his attention was needed unloading the wagons. She stopped at the kettle before she went to her wigwam.

As hungry as Damaris was, and as good-tasting as the food looked to be, she refused to allow the server to ladle

much of the stew into her wooden cup and went by herself
to the wigwam. She took a few bites and set her cup down
without wiping it. She flopped down and closed her eyes, for
she was completely spent.

Her cold feet woke her. She rolled over and saw that
the embers were almost out. It was entirely too dark in the
little hut to see if anyone else had come in. Common sense
told her that if Amie were in there, she would have stoked
up the fire.

Excerpt from the writings of Damaris Cooke,
1677 Massachusetts.

*I was alone in the wigwam. I hadn't slept as
long as it seemed. I heard voices waft through the
crisp night air. They created a strange echo that
gave an ethereal effect to the psalms that were being
sung at the campfire. I found the poignant music to
be most comforting.*

*I kindled the fire and it began to flicker and
flame. Yellow and orange danced up from a blue
base that hovered about the burning wood, and
its dreamy motion drew me back in time to the
summer of 1642. I remembered Jacob standing in
front of me wearing his linen nightshirt. It was our
wedding night. How naive I was at fifteen.*

*Remembering our first night together led sweet
tears to stream down the sides of my cheeks. I had
no power over my emotions when I allowed my
mind to bring me close to Jacob. I was able to recall
that magical night when my concerns were over-
come by natural enthusiasm. A passion for Jacob
burst into existence from then on; my fears were*

replaced with a sweet trust that carried Jacob and me through the years.

The night I learned Jacob had died, I told the Lord, "I have lived long and am ready to join Jacob in the hereafter." That's when I stretched myself out on the mat and placed my arms across my chest in a rest-in-peace sort of way. I closed my eyes and did my best to expel all the air from my lungs. I prayed, "If it were to be your will, take me out of this hateful, fearful, sinful world." Then I waited for God to do some sort of mystical transition from physical life into the spiritual realm.

Nothing like that happened. Minutes passed before I drew air back into my lungs and decided not to argue with God. Instead, my hand slipped underneath a rolled-up hide that I was using as a pillow and pulled out the Bible I had rescued from the Sassamon cabin. I opened it to one of Jacob's favorite scriptures, Isaiah 40:31:

"But they that wait upon the Lord shall renew their strength; they shall mount up with wings as eagles; they shall run and not be weary; and they shall walk and not faint."

I prayed, "Lord, please forgive me for my moment of foolish selfishness."

The next day, just about the whole camp turned out to hear John Eliot preach. The injured and crippled were brought in on bark cots. This was not the first time John Eliot had inspired the people. Every one of the praying Indian towns could trace its very roots back to the preaching of John Eliot. He had brought them all into a deeper understand-

*ing of the saving grace of the Lord Jesus Christ. It
was apparent to me that nothing was able to separate the praying Indians from the love of the Lord.
Not being burned out, not the freezing cold, not the
horrors of this escalating war—nothing.*

Damaris

Damaris awoke to the voice of the camp crier announcing
a meeting at the Council Fire. She pulled her blanket back
over her head.

Amie sat up. "John Eliot will not leave our encampment without preaching a sermon, even if today is the middle
of the week."

Damaris didn't respond. She couldn't bear to hear encouraging words right now. Amie pulled her wool blanket
from the bed, wrapped it over herself like a cloak. "I want to
stay as warm as I can."

Damaris didn't move.

Amie said, "I hear people outside." She snatched the
blanket off Damaris and held it up. "You need to come."

Damaris moved slowly, standing and letting Amie
wrap her in the blanket. She let Amie lead her to the gathering.

They stood in the circle waiting for John Eliot to begin
speaking. Damaris noticed that, even though his brown hair
had recently begun to show gray, it in no way distracted from
his gentle, kindly eyes—eyes that, to look into them, had
always been like looking into a soul that overflowed with
God's love.

Damaris turned away as a shiver passed through her. John found it difficult to sit still unless he had something constructive to do. She remembered how he loved to write about his missionary work in the Americas. Back in Namasket, when he came to work with John Sassamon, he would calm the very moment he sat down to write; that is when his pent-up energy would go directly through his writing implement and onto the paper.

Damaris was focused on John when she felt Amie's arm and blanket draw her into a silent, warm embrace. "He loves Jesus more than he loves himself." Amie whispered.

Grateful for her friend's presence, Damaris let the warmth seep into her heart. "He has survived grief. Perhaps I can learn from him how to go on," Damaris said.

Amie nodded and snuggled into the shared warmth. "He is not just talk. He truly believes the word of God and does his best to teach it and live it. It gives him joy." She took Damaris's hand. "It will bring you joy again, too."

John Eliot's sermon was about enduring through suffering. He used the story of Joseph from the book of Genesis, telling them Joseph had been betrayed by his very own brothers and how he spent thirteen years in a prison after he had been unjustly accused. "Joseph never took his eyes off the Lord and God's promises. You must do the same. In the end, Joseph was to be greatly blessed by God. And you will be, too."

When the sermon was over, Damaris had a burden on her heart that she wanted to share with the preacher. She waited patiently for the elders of the Natick to be the first to speak with him and was touched when the older men and women hugged and patted him on the back. One old woman even kissed him on the cheek.

Damaris was moved by the devotion and love between the preacher and his flock, especially in the pitiful camp on Deer Island. In spite of the suffering, she was blessed by the love that happened here, while on the outside, war raged.

After a time, Damaris captured her opportunity to communicate by walking the old shepherd back to his tent.

John Eliot's feet, together with hers, crunched through the snow. "Please accept my sincere condolences for your loss," he said. "Jacob was a good man. He will be missed."

"Yes, he was." Damaris's mind flashed to her thoughts from the night before. "He was a very good man," was all she said aloud.

They trudged a few more steps in silence before she changed the subject. "We are concerned that Amie could be killed or taken to be enslaved."

John Eliot was deep in thought before he answered. "There is a fort up north on the frontier near Fort Orange, where an effort is being made to provide a safe haven for Christian Indians of all tribes. Governor Andros has been working with Soquan and Moquan of the Mahicans to establish a peace council at Schaghticoke. It is a considerable distance north where the Hoosic and the Tomahanock rivers come together. The governor has put out the word of welcome to all the Christian tribes: Catholic and Puritan."

Damaris listened intently to John Eliot. "Do you believe this could be the right place for Amie to go?"

He glanced to the North. "Yes, I do. Governor Andros has graciously extended a personal invitation for me to bring refugees from my towns. It seems that the fur trade has suffered because of this war and people everywhere have felt the effects. Plymouth received word that the Mohawks declined Philip's invitation to fight against the English. The Delaware and Abenaki have said that they are willing to move toward a lasting peace. Reverend Fitch sent word to us that Uncas is making preparations to attend the peace council."

Damaris listened to everything John Eliot had to say. There was something he hadn't made clear, though. "But everyone here is waiting for the chance to go back to our own towns to rebuild. We want to rebuild. I've heard many others say that they are willing."

He continued to talk about the peace council as if she had not spoken. Then he said, "Amie has a very good chance to do well among the Mohawk."

Damaris could not hide the hope hidden beneath. "If you believe Amie will have a chance to start a new life, then that will be best." She stopped walking. Her shoulders slumped and her head bent forward. "I was not prepared for her to be taken that far away." She closed her eyes.

When Damaris looked up she noticed bright sunlight was striking against the white of the snow. The leafless hardwoods had a new look when they were covered with an inch of the fresh white stuff. "It is my prayer that we rebuild and begin to make a fresh start with our work for the Lord," the elder said, "but for right now, it does not look as though we will be rebuilding any too soon. I will make an effort to contact Uncas to see if he can provide a safe escort for Amie, someone who can guide her up to Schaghticoke. I should have some detailed information the next time I come with supplies."

When they arrived at the front of his tent, Damaris turned to face John Eliot and placed her arms about him, giving him a sincere hug. "Thank you for all that you do for us." Their eyes met. "I love you—you old saint." Her face turned toward where the refugees from his praying towns were camped. "We all love you."

When she turned to leave, he reached and stopped her at a half turn. "Damaris," his kind voice said, "The Lord will give you the strength you need when you need it and not before." He gently shook her shoulder before letting go. "Just remember Jacob is at peace with the Lord. Our lord Jesus is our only true stronghold and refuge." Before he disappeared into his old, stained tent, he turned to her once more. "You hold tight to God's promise, you hear?"

Damaris trudged back to the wigwam. She was not sure if she should tell Amie about the village up north, as it would mean that they would be separated. Right now, she didn't know if she could bear one more loss.

Chapter Twenty-Three

❧The Pung❧

Excerpt from the writings of Damaris Cooke,
1677 Massachusetts.

The war had escalated to the point that the
praying Indians absolutely could not leave Deer
Island without a colonial escort to vouch for them.
There was that much mistrust of Natives within
the colonies.

I remember how I cried out to God, "Give me
mercy," because I was afraid of the outside world.
The reports of the war's havoc beyond the gate were
frightful. Amie and I had been on Deer Island for
some time, and as bad as the refugee camp was for
its poor lodging and lack of regular meals, I had
become familiar with its daily routine and no one
there called me "wench" or made sinful, vile remarks.

———※———

January 1676

Amie

The snow fell long into the night the day before John
Eliot and the supply wagon came. It was one of those
quiet snows where the flakes were small and built up
over time, slow and steady.

Amie hung back while two women from Natick rushed to greet their husbands, who had returned with John Eliot. John stood on the buckboard, passing supplies down to his assistants. She watched him pass a sack of flour and a cask of molasses before he carefully handed down an unusually wide sled. She noticed John Eliot's eyes look from Damaris to her and back to Joseph Sipit, who reached up to take the sleigh.

It was an odd sort of sled. It was wider even than most toboggans. The Naticks put it to use right away to haul more reeds and firewood. Sharing the sleigh made it possible for the whole encampment to better scavenge needed materials.

Word was out around camp that she and Damaris were making preparations to leave the island. John Eliot's presence was a reminder that her time on Deer Island was almost up. Amie needed to settle her nerves from the rush of fear that leaving this place brought, so she wandered to the shore to see if some driftwood might have been washed up by the night's tide.

Amie felt an unusual warmness develop between her skin and leather dress the moment she was alone with her anxiety and anticipation. Finally, she fell to her knees and cried, "Lord, I am afraid to leave."

———⟿⟿———

That night, John Eliot called Amie and Damaris to come into his tent for a private meeting. They found him seated at a writing desk, where he had in front of him a few papers and a map. John did not fully look up. Instead, he motioned with his left hand for them to sit on the three-legged stools across from his portable table. His tin candleholders hung from the ridgepole and gave off a soft glow through cutouts in the metal. They flickered and danced about the walls of his canvas tent.

Amie stared at the candlelight and waited for him to speak. She waited as patiently as she could and watched the attention he gave to his papers. When her attention went back to the candlelight, her curiosity intensified. "What is that pattern supposed to be?" Her eyes remained on the light. "I have never seen such a thing."

He smiled and pointed his quill up toward the lantern. "What you see up there is the image of a fruit called the pineapple."

"Pine apple?" Amie looked at Damaris. "The pine apple is a curious-looking thing."

"The pineapple grows in a warm climate," Damaris piped. "They bring them up from the West Indies on the merchant ships."

Amie felt it peculiar the way John Eliot looked at her, then closed his eyes before he spoke. "Regular folks don't get to taste pineapples because they go straight away to the wealthy." He cleared his throat. "War captives are being sent to the West Indies on the return," he stated and turned back to his papers. "Right now we need to get down to the business of your travels."

John Eliot tapped the papers with his forefinger. "These are the details of the plan." His glance went from Amie to Damaris. "Amie, the way things are, you are not safe to travel unless you have an escort like Damaris or myself." He reached into his pocket and drew out a small bundle wrapped in a swatch of red wool, tied with a blue ribbon. He carefully untied it to reveal an oval of worked copper alloy. There was a design of a native woman holding an arrow in one hand and a bow in the other. Engraved patterns framed the central figure. The arrow in her right hand was pointed downward to signify that the intention was for peace. On the back were engraved the words:

At A COUNCIL,
Held at Charlestown, June the 20th 1676
In the present Warr with
The Heathen Natives of this Land.
they giving us peace and mercy
at there hands
Edward Rawson

"Amie, this medal is for you to keep with you at all times." John placed the peace medal into the palm of her hand, cupped his hands around hers, and closed her fingers around it. "It was not easy for me to get this for you, but, to me, it was worth the effort because this thing may save your life. It tells the soldiers that you are a praying Indian and not the heathen enemy. It has the potential to ensure your safe passage."

He reached back into his pocket and produced two short wampum belts that were identical in their design of a purple line going perpendicular with another line going horizontal across the middle. Located within each white quadrant was a pair of purple beads set together in such a way as to represent a point. "The purple symbol represents Uncas of the Mohegan," John explained.

John passed one of the belts to Amie and one to Damaris. "The same goes with these. When you arrive in Norwich, go directly to the Congregational Church. You will be met there by the Reverend Fitch and Thomas Leffingwell. You are to show them the wampum. This is how they will know that you are who you say that you are." His kind eyes gave Amie confidence that the men at the church in Norwich could be trusted. "Once you are with them, they will have all the rest figured out. Other praying Indians are with them now waiting for you." He looked at Amie. "They plan to leave for the Northern frontier after you arrive and the weather breaks."

John gathered up his maps and papers and placed them into a thin leather shoulder bag. "Damaris, do you agree to be Amie's colonial escort?"

"Yes."

John Eliot handed the bag to Damaris. "Godspeed."

The next morning, before Amie and Damaris had thought about starting their day, there was a rustle and a noise outside. Someone was at the door. Amie peeked out and saw two Natick men wearing colonial-style clothing outside of the lodge. "Where is sled?" one asked intently. Amie scrambled to get herself together before she moved the hide door cover aside.

These were the Indian men who had come in with John Eliot: Andrew Pittimee and James Speen. They were about ten years or so younger and were married to women from the Natick section of camp. Amie blushed because John Eliot had made a point to keep everyone away from that area for the first evening of their arrival. The old saint was considerate of the exiles from Natick.

John Speen and Andrew Pittimee were guides in the militia and were on temporary loan to John. About their necks, both wore peace medals exactly like the one that John had given to her last night. She thought it peculiar that she had not noticed the pendants before.

"We come to build for you a pung," Andrew said as he guided the sled away.

In about three days, the two men from Natick pulled the modified sled towards where the women pounded kernels of dried maize into flour. Amie almost dropped the four-foot wooden corn pounder when she looked up from her work and saw the finished project.

The pung looked like a pile of supplies but turned out to be a hidden, moving house made of bark panels, laced together to form a wigwam, lashed on top of the toboggan.

"You like pung?" Andrew asked, handing the leather pulls over to Amie. She took hold and gave a hard test yank. She thought it would be hard to move, but instead the pung stirred so quickly that Amie lost her balance and went plop, right into the snow. She landed on her backside and laughed. Damaris and the other women laughed with her.

There was room enough behind the hut to pack plenty of supplies. Their two black ash pack baskets would fit side by side quite nicely. There was a space made expressly for snowshoes, which they did not have. Then Amie decided to take a peek inside and discovered that there was more space in the interior than it looked like from the outside. Another curiosity she observed was that a stone mortar filled with sand had been set in the center on the floor underneath a movable elm bark smoke-hole cover. She and Damaris would be able to sleep on either side of a fire. The pung was the cleverest thing she had seen in a very long time—a bark-covered storage hut that was actually a moving house with the ability to build a fire inside. Amie began to feel much better about the decision to head out in the direction of the Mohegan.

A small group of women approached and handed Amie a pair of snowshoes. "We gift you these with prayers to God for your safe travel. We only wish we could spare more."

Mary Sipit, of the first Indians to come to Christ and live among the colonists, hugged Amie, then Damaris. She said, "Oh, Damaris, dear, you be very careful out there and take good care of our Amie. We will pray every day."

Amie opened her arms and hugged each one of the Natick women. "Thank you so much for the fine snowshoes. We are going to miss your good cheer and sense of humor. We love you."

Amie hugged Mary Sipit one more time. "You have a way of making the best of any circumstance." She tucked the snowshoes into their place on the pung. "Last night it rained enough to melt the top layer and freeze a crust of ice on top. If this condition holds, we should be able to move the pung along without much difficulty, except for our own fears and anxiety."

Chapter Twenty-Four

❧The Shadow Of Death❧

Amie

John Eliot secured the pung behind the supply wagon. "I will tow the sled as close as possible to where you are to meet Reverend Fitch," he said on his way out from behind. "No need for you to undergo any more hardship than necessary before I have to go in the other direction."

Amie and Damaris sat quietly on the wagon seat next to John Eliot. Amie's head turned this way and that to take in the surroundings.

After a time, Amie said, "The road here seems to be getting wider. Do you think we are getting close to a town?"

John nodded. "We will pass through what was Pawtucket."

Amie glanced about and felt the weight of the devastation the war had caused. Both the Wampanoag winter lodges and the colonial homesteads were left in ruins. Charred remains were all that was left in the aftermath of the conflict.

There were no smells of freshly baked bread, no men tending to their daily chores, no playful children, but rather a deep stillness screamed to be heard in the silent, eerie quiet where houses, barns, and pastures had been. The blanket of snow covering the places that had once bustled with life was undisturbed except for wild animal tracks.

When the wagon pulling the pung passed where Amie had spent time camping with her family in the early days, she became gloomy. "What has become of my Tispiquin?" The words broke from Amie in a mist of visible breath. "What has become of my husband?"

John Eliot heard Amie's trembling voice over the sound of the hooves and answered, "Last I heard, Philip is camped over at Assawompsett. I have no reports as to who is with him." Then he moved his arm in order to better point out the extent of burned-out camps and homesteads. "The ones who did this won't be back. There is nothing left to burn."

After a time he pulled up on the reins. "Whoa!" The horses stopped and there was dead silence except for a snort from their nostrils. Amie heard a bird call in the distance, then more silence. A horse pawed the snow.

John jumped down and dug around in order to expose the grass so that the horses could feed. Amie watched as he walked about to examine some of the trees. He stopped at a maple that had been purposely bent. He raised his hand and traced a carved design in its bark with his index finger before he looked up. "We will set up our camp here. This is where we are to wait for John and Andrew to return from their scouting."

Amie and Damaris jumped down from the wagon to help John Eliot set up camp. They had the fire going and the pottage cooked down by the time the scouts came in.

John Speen and Andrew Pittimee, the same two men from Natick who had built the pung on Deer Island, now wore tight-fitting leather leggings secured at the knee with woven wool ties. They were back to wearing breechclouts with loose-fitting tunic shirts cinched at the waist. Andrew carried a pipe tomahawk tucked in his wide, many-colored wool sash of arrowhead designs. John Speen had a mean-looking war club tucked into his blue-and-yellow woven waistband.

John Speen had just enough hair on the back of his head to tie a cluster of turkey feathers mixed with blue heron, red ribbon, and wampum strings that hung down from the feather cluster. The sight of them caused her to think of her husband. She remembered Tispiquin's outward appearance of warrior might, and blushed at a memory of his tenderness.

The guides' native clothing and red ocher paint caused them to look very different compared to how they had looked just a few days ago on Deer Island, when they brought the pung. She could see no sign of their peace medals.

Amie noticed that after the scouts had eaten they seemed anxious to take John Eliot aside for a private conference.

Damaris went into the pung, and Amie found herself sitting alone by the campfire. She stood up, rubbed the palms of her hands together, and held them out to feel the heat of the fire before she drew into her nostrils the delightful scent of the evening. She tipped her head back and considered how the night sky was filled with stars that went on and on and on into infinity. She felt very small and insignificant in comparison to the millions of twinkling stars.

Later the scouts joined her at the fire, where they listened to John Eliot quote two Psalms from the Algonquin Bible: Psalm 49 and Psalm 23. She knew the twenty-third by heart and spoke silently along with him in her language. "The Creator is my protector. He gives me rest in the meadow: he provides me quiet waters. He heals my being: he guides me on the trail of the good way for his name's sake. I may walk through many dangers, I will fear no bad thing: for the Creator of all things is with me; your weapon and walking stick they comfort me." John Eliot's voice was sensitive and soft when he said it in English. "Thou preparest a table before me in the presence of mine enemies: thou anointest my head with oil; my cup runneth over. Surely goodness and mercy shall follow me all the days of my life: and I will dwell in the house of the Lord for ever."

The twenty-third psalm was her favorite, but this night the words came alive and spoke directly to her like never before. In her heart, she thanked God for the comfort of His powerful Word.

The three men bunked in the wagon. On their first night in the pung, Amie and Damaris were anxious to see how the inside fireplace was going to work. It was a little smoky at first, but the air cleared as soon as Amie adjusted the smoke-hole covering. Amie spoke once they had settled into their bedrolls. "It was about thirty-five years ago when my family wintered here in this place. I remember my mother wanted one of the cast iron kettles like the Plymouth women had." For the first time in a while, Amie's eyes twinkled in the firelight. "Mother would mention this to Massasoit so often that by the next winter he had brought her a very large one. That pot Father traded for was big enough to make corn soup for the whole camp." She brought her hand up to cover her mouth when she laughed, then added, "I'm not persuaded it was the size kettle my mother had in mind for herself." Amie laughed.

Damaris blurted, "You sure looked funny when you first tugged on the pung." Then Damaris snorted and giggled till she passed gas.

Amie didn't know if it was because they were finally out of Deer Island, or what, but she and Damaris became giddy and laughed uninhibited into the wee hours of the night.

The dawn was near when Amie had an urge to go. The fire was practically out. She looked at what was left of the coals and decided that she would bring some wood when she came back.

The dawn air was not as crispy cold as she had expected. When she looked up, she could no longer see the stars and felt it might soon snow.

Amie chose to hide behind some bushes a few feet from camp in case one of the men might come out of the wagon. She had no sooner squatted down when she heard the sounds of movement in the distance. From what she could tell there was a party of perhaps a dozen or so riding towards camp at a pretty good pace. Frightened, Amie passed on getting the firewood and moved quickly back into the pung. Her heart beat fast, and she could hear it thump in her ears. She felt a pang of dread when she realized she was safely inside the pung but had neglected to awaken the men in the wagon. Just then she heard their voices and the sounds of metal and wood as a musket ball was being rammed into a barrel. She gave a sigh of relief and thanked God they were braced.

"What is going on?" Damaris asked as she rose from her furs and rubbed her eyes.

Amie pointed in the direction of the commotion. "I hear some riders. Listen, there must be at least twenty or so."

"I hear them."

Amie didn't know why she whispered. The riders were not close enough to hear her voice. "Let's lay low." She got herself back under her covers and listened to the clatter get louder and peeked over at Damaris, who was peeking back.

They waited.

Once the riders arrived, Amie tried to make out who was speaking. "I think it is the militia."

Amie heard, "Captain Church sent us." The voice was coming from the man in charge. He was speaking to John Eliot. Then she heard the same voice command, "What is that?" She was sure he was referring to the pung.

Amie had closed the smoke flap so that the sled looked like it was carrying a normal load. She heard John Eliot say, "Supplies."

"Soldier, check it out," came a blaring command.

Amie and Damaris could see the business end of a rifle being inserted between the door pole and the deer hide that protected them.

Suddenly the door flap was flung open. Damaris froze motionless at the sight of the soldier's face.

The young militiaman's mouth dropped. Amie knew he could not believe what he was seeing because Francis looked utterly shocked.

Damaris was face-to-face with her son.

Amie's heart raced and her mind spun as she watched Damaris move her hand around to signal to Francis not to reveal what he was seeing.

"What is in there, Boy?" A husky voice rang out.

Francis's eyes moved from his mother to Amie and back to Damaris. "Uh...not much, Sir, just some blankets and such."

The flap closed as quickly as it had opened. Amie could hear the men's voices fading in and out of her audible range. "...reconnaissance...at...fort...tomorrow...your presence... the scouts...necessary...Captain Church." Then the sound of their voices faded into a subdued murmur and she could not make out any more of their words. Amie felt around, found a small piece of birch bark, and rolled the bark into the shape of a cone. She fitted the pointy end of the cone into her ear and leaned her head over to listen through the wall. Her forehead furrowed and her eyes moved to the left and upwards in intense concentration.

> *Excerpt from the writings of Damaris Cooke, 1677 Massachusetts.*
>
> *The militiamen were out there for what seemed a very long time.*
>
> *While Amie was busy listening in on the militia, my heart felt great joy after my brief encounter with Francis. Even now I feel it, as I think that only a thin layer of bark and woven matting was all that separated me from him. I remember that I closed my eyes and listened to the murmur of the men's voices and hoped to hear Francis. I regret that I did not pay attention to Amie and her use of the birch-bark eavesdropping device. Instead I closed my eyes to remember the way Francis's dark, wavy hair had curled up on either side of his wool military cap. I was thinking about his broad forehead and deep-set brown eyes.*
>
> *The moment I heard the rumble of the hooves, I let out a sigh, flopped over to my back, and kicked up my feet with joy.*

Damaris

Damaris rolled back and rose to support her weight on her elbows. She placed her chin in her hand. "Did you see the expression on Francis's face?" Then her heart deflated like a rotten squash when she saw Amie's glaring eyes and tightened lips.

"Tispiquin has been executed," Amie said.

"Are you sure you heard right?"

Amie did not answer. The silence was so loud Damaris felt it pound like the beat of war drums.

Amie

Unexpected anger flared through Amie at being trapped in the confines of the pung. "He was executed," she blurted, then rolled over to bury her head.

Amie felt the light pressure of Damaris's hand upon her shoulder and was thankful that her friend did not speak. Damaris's touch was a comfort. She stayed on her tummy. "He turned himself in about a month ago in order to gain my freedom. He was waiting for Captain Church to arrive, when some soldier decided to see if the rumors were true."

Amie rolled back over. "Captain Church told everybody Tispiquin was bulletproof, and some doltish fool shot him." Amie dropped herself face down and went silent.

Excerpt from the writings of Damaris Cooke, 1677 Massachusetts.

Just about everything we held dear, just about everything we had known had been ripped away by this terrible war. We were in the middle of the wilderness heading into the unknown. The wound of losing Jacob re-opened wide in my heart when Amie heard the news about Tispiquin's execution.

Trapped in the pung, we bled inside each other's wounds.

———

Amie rolled back. "Your son-in-law, John Rickard, was out there with the militia. I recognized his voice. He is the one who held that Tispiquin was executed. He said that Captain Church made an attempt to save Tispiquin but he didn't get back to Plymouth in time. Maybe it was an accident. Maybe it was on purpose. Either way, my husband is gone." Her face felt stiff. "Many Wampanoag, Narragansett, and Pequot are being sent as slaves on ships to the West Indies."

She sighed. "Ninigit still lives. He and his mother were among the prisoners."

"When my father was Ninigit's age, he was indentured to serve on an English ship." Damaris probably meant the story to be comforting. "A tempest broke up the vessel and he had to survive in the West Indies. He told us there is warm weather and plenty of wild pigs and chickens and no one gets mad if you hunt them."

Amie sat up and put on her moccasins. "I heard Francis tell John Rickard that he had been to Massachusetts Bay to check in on his baby sister Ruth. She is doing well." Amie's bloodshot eyes rose. "Mary is keeping my Betty safe in Plymouth." After she had shared what news she had heard, Amie lifted the pung's door flap. "I want to take a walk alone."

She thought to herself, "Truth is, I want to go deep into the woods, bury myself in the snow, and freeze to death. I have heard it is a good way to die."

Chapter Twenty-Five

❧On Their Own❧

Excerpt from the writings of Damaris Cooke, 1677 Massachusetts.

I have liked the taste of compressed Chinese tea ever since my father was able to carry tea in his shop. I remember the creatures called dragons that were embossed on the blocks. He told me dragons didn't exist in real life. Even to this day I know little about the world outside of Plymouth, Massachusetts Bay, and Namasket.

We camped where Amie's family had wintered, so I knew she was familiar with the place, but the deeply wooded area was all new to me. The trees were thick, with much underbrush surrounding the large clearing. We had set up camp on the outer edge. There was evidence that it had been used many winters over. Indications of campfires past were here and there, making what appeared to be a circle. Not far from where the wagon was parked, a stack of bark sheets that had been spared from the carnage were ready to be used to cover the winter wigwams.

Amie's ancestors had come to this place for many a year to spend the winter months. I could see the sense of it because the campground was well protected from the high winds by the hills and trees.

*These same trees provided good-burning hardwood
to keep the fires going.*

Damaris

Damaris emerged from the pung to find John Eliot and the scouts sitting around a small fire enjoying a sweet-smelling hot drink. Perhaps they had made a trade with the soldiers for a block of tea. She hoped there would be enough for her.

Damaris absorbed the warmth of the campfire, wiggled her rag-wrapped toes inside her moccasins, and looked at John Eliot. "This wood is superior to the scrub wood we could scrounge at Deer Island. I pray for our friends who still remain there."

Andrew stared at the flames. "I pray to Lord Jesus. He bring the time of the song bird's return early this turtle's back."

Damaris drew her feet back. Heat surged through her wrapped feet when the leather made contact and it felt good. "Do I smell Chinese tea?"

"Yes, it is." John poured her a cup before Andrew turned in, leaving Damaris alone with John Eliot. The tin cup felt warm and comforting in her hand. She savored the nostalgic aroma before she took a sip.

When Damaris looked up from her cup, it seemed to her that John Eliot was patiently waiting to speak to her about something. She set the tea aside in order to give him her undivided attention. "What is on your mind?"

John Eliot's eyes closed and his head dropped. When he lifted it back up he reached over and put another chunk of ash wood on the fire. "Damaris, we are in a dreadful time;

a time that tries our very souls, tests our faith, and the two of you must trust in the Lord to help you carry on in spite of suffering. We have no right to give in to our grief right now. God would want us to persevere and do whatever we can to improve the lives of our loved ones."

Damaris felt comfort from the tea as it began to soothe the inner trauma that yearned to become numb.

"I would very much like to be able to escort you all the way to Reverend Fitch, but it is time for me to return to the action. This is as far as the scouts and I dare to go. There are more supplies we desperately need to bring to Deer Island." He paused. "Do you still have the papers I gave you?"

"Yes." Damaris lifted her eyes. "There are enough supplies on board the pung and it is not much farther for us to go." She tilted her head upwards. "We are in good hands with our Lord Jesus. God willing, Amie and I shall be safe with Reverend Fitch in a day or two."

The moment Damaris mentioned the precious name of Jesus, John's shoulders dropped a bit.

"Thank you for reminding me of whose we are," he said.

The following morning the men from Natick provided fresh-cooked meat. Damaris drank another cup of tea and observed Amie's quiet resolve at breakfast.

With the map in hand, Damaris stood near Amie to watch the wagon disappear into the forest. The two word-lessly waited next to the pung until the sound of the horse and wagon faded away.

There was stillness, with the exception of the wind-song through the branches above. Amie broke the silence. "Who is pulling the pung? You or me?"

"I will," Damaris said. Because she was the first to pull, she strapped on the snowshoes to help her draw the pung over the deep snow. She tugged twice before their sled released and began to move. They trekked steady in a south-westerly direction.

As the time wore on, the daylight penetrated through the evergreens as well as the naked branches of huge elms and other hardwoods. The afternoon sun shone in sections beneath the branches. The light moved like a rhythmic dance as it reflected within the canopy. The sunshine drove away the gloom of dark shadows and kept them from falling across the trail.

After a time, they began to sing Psalms, then Amie started to chant one of the working songs of her tribe. It was one she had taught Damaris when they were picking berries as girls. Damaris was pleasantly surprised that the vocables come back to her.

The song's poetic rhythm helped them to lift one foot up out of the snow and sink it in front, keeping them moving for a longer period of time. They made good progress with the pung. "If we keep up this pace, we might be in Norwich sooner than I had expected."

Damaris noticed Amie was looking to the west where the sun had started to fade. "We best think about where to set up camp."

She smelled smoke from a fire long before a little cabin came into view. Her heart felt a hint of hope and even joy at the site of the cabin and outbuildings. It was the first time since they left the colony that they had seen a home that was unharmed by the ravages of the war. "Reverend John Eliot said there would be fewer signs of devastation the closer we come to Norwich," Amie said.

The tiny windows of the log cabin were illumined with a warm, yellow glow. Damaris thought about how cozy it might be inside. She visualized herself seated comfortably on one side of the hearth and Amie on the other with a warm bowl of pottage in their hands like they had done so many times in Namasket. Their men had often been away from home for days, giving time for the women and children to gather together at each other's cabins. In Damaris's nostalgic moment, she gave herself permission to enjoy the fond memories of the communal praying town.

They parked their pung far enough away as to not alarm the people living there, but close enough that they could run to them should any trouble come in the night.

Damaris was pleased with the camping place, and as soon as they were able to get settled, she reached into her pack basket and brought out a bag containing cakes wrapped in cornhusks. They were made with parched grandmother corn that had been pounded into coarse flour and then mixed with dried berries and fat. After a long day's trek, the corn bar tasted good. By eating this way, they were less likely to draw attention to themselves. The corn cakes required no cooking. Damaris chose not to eat too much too fast, because the food would expand. She remembered to drink liquid and passed the water keg to Amie.

Later, inside the pung, Damaris watched Amie build a small fire. She was able to get embers to the point of glowing with very little smoke by using resin-infused sticks.

Amie looked up from her work. "I saved the heartwood until now because it is quick-starting and has smokeless qualities." She carefully slid the remaining precious pieces back into her basket.

Before she fell asleep, Damaris closed her eyes and thanked God for the day. She prayed that she and Amie would be spared any more brokenheartedness.

Chapter Twenty-Six

The Bear

Damaris

Damaris woke up from her dream about dragons in China to the sound of a commotion going on outside. The door flap swung open and Amie dove through a spray of snow. "I saw a bear," she exclaimed.

"It is winter. Bears are sleeping, Amie, you know that."

"The bear saw me." Her eyes widened, her voice raised a pitch level, and she took hold of Damaris's arm.

She strained to listen and heard heavy breathing outside.

"Did you hear that? It's out there," Amie said.

The pressure of Amie's fingers hurt Damaris's arm. "I am afraid to look." She believed that Amie saw a bear. Even though she knew that bears rarely came out of hibernation early, it had been known to happen when they were very hungry.

They heard loud breathing and sniffing outside the door. Damaris felt around for her knife.

Amie let go her grip on Damaris and picked up the war club. She nodded towards Damaris's knife. "If the bear sticks its head through the door, I'll club it with the pagami-gon, you slit its throat."

They sat at the ready when suddenly the big black creature stuck its head through the door hole. Amie hesitated for a split second, then she hit the big head of the animal with the club.

As soon as Amie's weapon fell, Damaris's brain told her that what Amie hit was not a bear. She set down her knife and drew in a quick breath. "It is a dog," she exclaimed. Jacob had told her once about seeing a breed of dog called a Newfoundland. He'd said it was as big as a bear, but she hadn't thought such a thing possible until now. "I have never seen such a large dog."

The canine, now partially in and mostly outside the pung, was the same size as a respectable black bear. Damaris looked down at the still creature. Actually the head she was looking down on was bigger than any black bear she had seen.

"Did I kill it?" Amie asked.

Damaris moved her hand down toward the big black nose and felt warm breath. "It's still alive. Unconscious, but very much alive."

Once they had the Newfoundland's mouth tied shut with a leather thong, Amie said to the dog, "I'm so sorry. I didn't mean to hurt you."

Damaris placed her hand gently on its head and checked for blood. She spoke in an attempt to reassure the creature. "You are going to be alright."

Just then they heard snowshoe clatter outside, and a masculine voice asked, "What is this thing? I heard a voice. Is there someone in there? What have you done to my Hurit?"

"We thought it was a bear," Amie said.

Damaris lifted the fur flap of the door for the man so that he could come close to his dog.

"I am very sorry, sir," Amie said.

The man maneuvered his upper torso though the small opening of the pung to get closer to the dog's injured head. His hardy fingers touched his dog, softly moving the thick hair aside so that he could better diagnose the wound. "Hurit, Hurit—old girl." He spoke softly to the dog. "You are going to be all right." He gently stroked Hurit's fur. He checked her over and untied the thong. "These two old women were afraid of you. They thought you were a bear," he laughed quietly.

Damaris took from Amie's tight lips and wrinkled nose that she felt somewhat offended that this man thought of her as an old woman. She looked closer at the man and could see that he was more than a decade younger than they were. His face was strong-featured, with a long scar that ran across his left cheek from the high point of its bone to near the bottom of his ear. His skin tone was light, yet he dressed in leather leggings and a breechclout. His long, brown, wavy hair hung loose from his wool voyager cap. His capote was made from a white wool blanket that had blue, yellow, and red stripes along the bottom edge. He had it cinched with a matching wool sash.

Damaris saw the dog blink and look up at the man. He petted her again before he turned from Hurit. "She'll pull through." He gave the dog another gentle pat. "Allow me to introduce myself. I am Thomas Leffingwell. And just who are you and why are you squatting on my land?"

The sound of Damaris's heart throbbed in her ear all the while she stared at the scar on Thomas's face and her mind repeated the name *Thomas Leffingwell*.

Thomas Leffingwell was the name she'd heard at the meeting with John Eliot. She gently stroked the fur of the injured dog who belonged to the very person who held their fate in his hands. She was close to feeling completely defeated when a scripture came into her head: "'Fear not for I am with thee' sayeth the Lord." She remembered the satchel with the strange woven wampum belt and message for Reverend Fitch that John Eliot had given her.

Damaris reached for the leather bag. "We are friends of John Eliot and I, uh, I have instructions and such in this satchel." She held her hand on the flap of the bag. "My friend and I are on our way to Norwich to give a message to the Reverend Fitch." She looked down at the leather container and back up at the man with the scar. "Are you the Mr. Leffingwell who is friends with the Reverend Fitch?" She shifted the pouch over onto her lap and placed both of her hands on top of the flap. "The Reverend Fitch who is a friend of the Reverend John Eliot?"

Thomas gave a quick glance toward the leather bag in Damaris's lap, then he turned his attentions back to his dog. "I'm well acquainted with the work of John Eliot."

Damaris lifted the flap and then put it back down. "I have some papers from Reverend Eliot that I have been instructed to bring to the Congregational Church in Norwich. They concern my friend and also the fate of the people who are at Deer Island. Reverend Eliot said that Reverend Fitch has some connections up in the North Country who may be able to help us."

Thomas patted the dog and did not look up. "I understand that you are concerned for your friends, but right now, can I invite you two to lend me a hand? I need to bring Hurit to my cabin," he said.

"Hurit means beautiful," Amie said.

Damaris looked down at the dog and petted her. "She is very beautiful."

"Once we get to the cabin, I'm sure my wife, Mary, will be happy to give you women something to eat. Then there will be time for us to have a good look at your papers."

He looked from Amie to Damaris. "But first let me get you settled inside where it is warm." After saying this, he turned to poor Hurit who was still halfway in and halfway outside of the pung. "How about we see if we can get the old girl all the way into the hut so I can pull her home?"

Damaris gave a smile of assurance in Amie's direction. "My heart is thankful to know that the cozy cabin belongs to the very person, Thomas Leffingwell, whom John Eliot sent us to meet. My mother always said, 'Trust in the Lord with all your heart and lean not on your own understanding, and He will make your paths straight.'"

She looked intently at Amie. "I believe God sent the bear dog."

Chapter Twenty-Seven

⚜Mary Uncas Leffingwell⚜

Amie

The inside of the cabin was every bit as warm and welcoming as the way Damaris had said she imagined it to be. Amie leaned in to Damaris's ear. "This is much roomier than what we lived in back in Namasket." She sat at the table and watched Damaris walk over to the fireplace.

The fireplace was made of fieldstone and had a wooden mantle above the hearth. The fire crackled and snapped when Thomas set two logs on it. "This is my wife, Mary Uncas Leffingwell," he said. After the introductions, he left the room.

The walls of the cabin were adorned with familiar items, such as a white ash bow with a bark quiver full of arrows. Useful items hung from hooks, including three split-ash pack baskets and wool coats fashioned from trade blankets. The windows were covered with homespun curtains. Above the fieldstone hearth hung the longest-barreled firearm Amie had ever seen. The Leffingwells had several belts made of the purple and white shell beads. One in particular was the same design as the ones that she and Damaris had been given by John Eliot. She felt for the bag that held hers.

Amie's eyes focused on Mary. There was something familiar about her. She would have been just a child the last time they'd met, but now she had a few gray hairs showing against the chestnut brown of her well-groomed single braid bound at the nape of her neck.

When Mary's back was to Amie, she admired the six-inch leather truss embellished with both beads and flattened quills in her hair. At its base, two ribbons hung down to the middle of her back, partially covering the braid. When she turned back around, Amie realized Mary's skin tone was a lighter shade than her own, more the shade of Damaris in the summertime. Excitement warmed her heart. She knew for certain who the woman was. Would she remember their time together?

Mary's eyes became penetrating as she looked at her guests. "I have heard that there is still much trouble with the Narragansett and the Wampanoag back east from where you have come."

Amie felt tears in her eyes. "Damaris and I have lost our husbands in this war. Our little town was attacked and burned." She propped her head in her hands with her elbows on the table. "I was taken to Deer Island." She smiled through teary eyes at Damaris. "Damaris here arranged for her daughter to indenture at an inn at Massachusetts Bay so that she would be safe while her mother came to help me."

Mary tilted her head while she listened to Amie, then glanced over to Damaris. "You are courageous." Then she looked back to Amie. " Do you know what is to become of the people on Deer Island?"

Damaris walked over to join them at the table. "That is John Eliot's concern as well. Conditions are very bad on that island. We were cold and hungry. That is part of our mission in finding Reverend Fitch. John Eliot has heard that there is a new praying town being established up north at Schaghti-coke on the frontier, where conditions will be much better, at least until we can return to rebuild our old town."

The space between Mary's eyebrows furrowed. "The militia are not following you, are they?" She looked more closely at Amie. "I believe I know who you are." She frowned. "You are King Philip's sister." Her eyes flashed. "I don't want any trouble to follow you here. My father, Uncas, has made it very clear that the Mohegan don't want to become involved in this conflict with the English."

Mary Uncas Leffingwell and Amie sat and stared at each other for a very long time, neither speaking.

Finally Amie broke the silence. "I want you to know that I do not support Metcomet in this war. He deserves respect and freedom to lead the Wampanoag and I honestly believe that he was working out his conflicts with the colonial government. If only my son-in-law, John Sassamon, would have been given more time, between them, they could have resolved much." Amie shifted in her seat. "When the Pequot and Narraganset, my father's enemies, began to call him King Philip, I am afraid this caused Philip to become full of pride."

"What is happening with the war now?" Mary Leffingwell asked.

"The last word we heard was that the colonial militias were gaining control and had rounded up Wampanoag, Pequot, and Narraganset prisoners. I heard that militiamen have taken Phillip's wife, Wootenekanuske, and son, Ninigit, to the prison camp and that they are going to send the prisoners down to the West Indies to be sold as slaves."

Thomas Leffingwell appeared in the doorway of the back room where the dog was recuperating. "Hurit is doing much better."

Mary's eyes went from her husband back to Amie before she said, "I hear that many people have died on both sides of this war." Mary's voice softened. "The way people are blaming your brother, I'm surprised you got away."

Amie's voice rose. She looked to Damaris and back to Mary. "John Eliot came up with a plan and asked Damaris if she was willing to help." Amie gestured with hand motions toward Damaris's satchel. Her upper body slumped down before she pushed herself back upright. "Damaris and I agreed I should take my chances with the plan of Governor Andros that Reverend Fitch is able to help with."

"I'm aware of this peace council. Word of it is spreading to the neutral tribes." Mary turned her head to Amie. "How did you find out about the captives?"

"We were hiding in the pung when the militiamen came into camp. Damaris and I couldn't hear their words so I made a cone from birch bark to put up against the wall and that is when I heard them saying that our people who were aiding Philip and those who were not at Deer Island under guard would become prisoners to be shipped away." Amie's eyes opened wider. "It crossed my mind to try and hide out with neutral tribes, but mistrust is everywhere. I do not want to be sold as a slave to the West Indies."

Amie had her hand on the royal blue ribbon that held the medallion and had already pulled it up from where it was concealed beneath her overblouse. She lifted the peace medal over her head to hand it to Thomas Leffingwell.

By this time, Damaris had retrieved the purple and white shell-woven belt that held the symbols of the Mohegan. She handed wampum across the table to Mary and watched the Mohegan woman's pointer finger extend and move over the tubular shell weaving.

Mary looked up and gave Damaris a gentle smile. "Here is the center of our Mohegan unity under my father,

Uncas, and over here it shows that we are a separate nation from the Pequot. This is the new symbol of my people, created when my father made an agreement to become friends with the English."

When Amie handed Thomas the peace medallion, the words flew out of her like an arrow flying from the straining string of a bow just released.

"I didn't know on what side my husband Tispiquin would choose to fight. All I remember is that he was acting out of the ordinary ever since the murder of our daughter's husband, John Sassamon. Tispiquin was in the middle between my brother and the court. He tried to prevent the conviction of Tobias. He was convinced the Wampanoag were innocent. He put up bail. He sold all his western lands in order to get the funds to do it. I tried to talk him out of selling his land, but Tispiquin would hear nothing of it. He rarely became angry, but that day he became angry with me and Betty as well. The court came down with the verdict of guilty."

Amie's eyes widened, her delivery sped up, and she waved her hands about as she was talking. "Betty and I had no reason to think that the eyewitness, Patuckson, would lie. He testified under oath that he witnessed the murder."

She finally took in some air. "Plymouth wasted no time in bringing my brother's men to the gallows. We are still suffering from everything that has been happening to our family ever since the murder and hanging that sparked the war." She sighed. "When Wampapaquin's noose broke during the hanging process, Tispiquin believed in his heart that it was a sign that his friends were innocent." She looked toward Damaris and back to Mary Uncas. "I could feel it in my innermost being, that is why Tispiquin left home right after the execution of Tobias. He went off with my brother. They were in a fury. When Tispiquin did not return home that night, I knew that he had participated in the violence on Swansea. The men were fired up that night." Her eyes became like that of a dog who had been punished for something it didn't do. "I know Tispiquin did not want an all-out war."

Damaris added to their story. "We thought Swansea might be enough. They would blow off some steam and that would be the end of it. But things went from bad to worse in very short order. Men from Plymouth went out to try to settle things down and before they got there, they found murdered bodies on the road. One of the bodies had been cut in the stomach and a Bible stuffed inside." Damaris's eyes teared when she gave the report.

Amie felt the same pain as when her childhood pet was slaughtered for the pot at the thought that Tispiquin was present for the Swansea attack. "We weren't sure who we could or could not trust," she said. "They executed Tispiquin in Plymouth, and I'm never going to see my husband again." Amie looked at the Leffingwells. "Damaris's husband was killed in the Connecticut valley."

Amie brought her hands up to her chin to support her downcast countenance. "Captain Church had promised Tispiquin that his life would be spared, but that is not what happened. When he was captured, they killed him before Captain Church was able to get back to Plymouth to defend him. Some of the militia have gone fanatical. They aren't showing mercy or justice to the captives. If they even think that someone might be on King Philip's side, they are put among those being sent away in slavery without a trial. Deer Island is about the only safe place for Christian Natives, and being there is worse than being a prisoner. We know first-hand. We were there just three days ago."

Thomas held the Mohegan wampum before he passed it back to Damaris. "Wannalancet told me he had heard about the retaliations on Indians and that is why he was hard pressed not to strike back when his village was attacked." He picked up the peace medal and examined the polished oval carefully before he passed it to his wife.

Mary handed it back to Amie. "My father will be able to help you." She gave a nod of support. "We can head out that way tomorrow."

Amie breathed a sigh. "I hope so. I don't know where I can be safe. I don't want to be sent away as a slave. I don't want to be executed. I have had no part in what my brother has done. All we have tried to do is to help him to understand that everything around us is changing."

Suddenly Damaris said, "John Sassamon did not deserve to die. All he ever did was to help our communities." Her lips pursed. "He had no choice but to warn Plymouth. Amie and I know that what he reported about Philip amassing arms was true." She looked toward Thomas. "Amie and I saw how many guns Tobias was trading for."

"Yes, what Damaris said is true, three years ago," Amie sighed. "We were concerned then, but Tispiquin and I never agreed with the law against Indians owning guns and decided not to do anything about it." She looked toward Damaris. "At that time, Damaris and I saw Philip in Plymouth. We heard him promise that he would let the Plymouth magistrates handle the land problems."

———※———

Damaris

"That is when the trouble could have ended, but it seems Philip could not work out his differences and our praying towns had to suffer for it." After Damaris said that, she began to realize that her words caused Amie's eyes to tear, so she went and knelt by the chair, put her arm around Amie's back with one hand and held her hand with her other. "God will see you through all this. I believe God will, but for now it seems right for us to grieve our losses."

Amie leaned her head against Damaris's shoulder and wept.

Still holding tight to her friend, Damaris turned her focus back to the Leffingwells. "During our time at Deer Island, Amie was stoic. She held herself together in order to help the others to survive. But now that we are in a safe place with you, Mary, now that Amie has a full belly and a warm, cozy fire, she is finally able let down her guard." Damaris's eyes widened and her mouth formed a partial smile. "Thank you both so much for giving us a blessing like this, but especially for Amie."

Mary Uncas Leffingwell rose up from her seat and walked behind them, placing her hands on Amie's tense shoulders and beginning to knead with her fingers. "My father, Uncas, will help you," she promised as her nimble fingers located knots. "Do you not remember when our people camped together? I was a little child? It was the winter of the broken-winged goose. You were in charge of me and some of the other children. Remember when we would sneak out to feed the injured goose?"

Damaris felt Amie surrender to the pressure of Mary's fingers. "I remember that her mate would not abandon her. We fed the geese and kept the secret for almost a moon."

"Oh yes, but then," Mary lifted her hands and came around to face Amie.

"But then we got caught," Amie said, and the room went silent.

Damaris broke in as she got up from the floor and took a seat. "I am curious about the geese. What happened?" The two of them glowered at her simultaneously. Damaris felt assaulted.

Amie's cheeks rose as her mouth pursed. "It was a very harsh winter. They killed the geese for the kettle." Amie's facial expression softened toward Damaris. "Remember my telling you the story about my mother's really large community kettle Massasoit brought to her? The one I spoke to you about the other night?"

"Yes."

Mary Uncas pulled out a chair to sit next to Amie and said, "That was the biggest kettle I have ever seen, before or since. Whatever happened to it?"

"Philip had it, last I knew," Amie said. "He took over the tribe after our older brother died."

"Do you remember the Abenaki silversmith?" Mary asked Amie.

Damaris watched Mary feel the front of her blouse. So did Amie, because they each wore an identical silver brooch. It was something that Damaris did not share, but she was glad to see Mary draw Amie's mind away from the war.

Chapter Twenty-Eight

✄Damaris's Attitude Adjustment✄

Damaris

Since there was nothing she could contribute to Amie and Mary's reunion, Damaris said, "I'm going into the back room to check on Hurit." Before she left the room, she paused at the door to observe the two, face to face, not taking notice of or responding to her words. Now that they'd found the Leffingwells, Amie would be going back to her people. She could feel Amie slipping away from her.

Thomas was sitting by the hearth, reading over John Eliot's papers. Amie was lost in memories that she shared only with Mary, and Damaris felt like she was needed in the room about as much as a weevil in a corn cake. "I better check on the dog," she said.

She had never seen a dog so big that it could have been mistaken for a bear before. The gentle creature looked up at Damaris with big, wide-set eyes that seemed to say, "I forgive you." Which was exactly what she would have wanted to hear if the creature could talk.

Hurit nuzzled while Damaris stroked her long, thick fur. The hefty canine's broad head rested on Damaris's lap. The Newfoundland's black nose felt wet to the touch. Damaris checked Hurit's head where the pagamigon had struck and found that it didn't seem that it had done much harm, other than to knock her out for a time. Plus, the dog seemed to be in its right mind. That was a good sign.

"If it is all the same to you, sweet girl, I'd rather stay for a while in the back room with you." Damaris looked toward the door that led to the other room and petted the dog. "I was feeling a bit out of place." Her new friend nudged her with her cold nose, let out warm breath, and wagged her tail to indicate she was welcome to continue with the attention.

Damaris felt comforted as she stroked the creature. She closed her eyes and petted the dog's fur. She remembered the times when Jacob would allow her to stroke his hair.

Excerpt from the writings of Damaris Cooke, 1677 Massachusetts.

Oh, how I loved that man. Jacob was the closest thing to Jesus that I had ever known this side of heaven. I closed my eyes and played memories of him over in my mind. I missed him so.

The voices in the other room were full of laughter. Thomas had returned to the table and, as their voices rose, part of me wanted to join in with them, but I didn't feel as though I fit. The truth was, I didn't want be there at all. I wanted to go back to the days before the murder of John Sassamon and the outbreak of war. All I wanted was to be back in my life just the way it was only a short while before the war, when Jacob had his head in my lap and I was stroking his hair.

As I write this, I recall the feel of the warm tears that streamed down the side of my face and how I did nothing to stop the continuous flow of them. Somehow, as I rode out the waves of emotion of that moment, I sensed the closeness of my savior and remembered that Jesus suffered more sorrow than I would ever be able to imagine when he died on the cross for me. It was well with my soul in spite of all the suffering I had faced those past few months, and the suffering I suspected was yet to come.

I remembered when I was a young girl, my mother would make me memorize scriptures, and there were times, before the Lord became truly real to me, that I must confess that I wasn't always keen on it. Then Philippians 4:4 came to mind: "Rejoice in the Lord always: and again I say Rejoice. Let your moderation be known to all men. The Lord is at hand. Be careful for nothing; but in everything by prayer and supplication with thanksgiving let your requests be made unto God. And the peace of God, which passeth all understanding, will keep your hearts and minds through Christ Jesus."

There had been considerable commotion surrounding the dog and the Leffingwells. Damaris realized that she had neglected to bring in the Bible, one of the few treasures that she had brought with her. Hurit hastened her thoughts into action by nudging to be let outside.

After retrieving the Bible from the pung, Damaris stood at the door and waited for Hurit. She breathed deeply of the fresh evening air. The dog charged around in the moonlit snow. Although she wasn't romping with Hurit, she felt a new sense of well-being, encouragement, and inner peace rise up within. For the first time since she and Amie arrived at this place, Damaris felt calm, rested, and ready to face the next part of their journey, now that she had renewed her mind from worry. She heeded the voice of her mother, who had warned her many times that worry was a sin against God.

Damaris brought Hurit in, settled back with the dog on the bearskin rug, and started what she called her "thank list."

She was blessed to see Francis, and he looked healthy and well.

She thanked God that Ruth was well.

She was thankful that Mary had opened her home in Plymouth to Betty Sassamon. She was proud of her daughter.

She was thankful to God that Amie was in a safe place, and she prayed the Lord Jesus would continue to see them safe.

Damaris drifted off to sleep on the fur rug with Hurit in her arms and thanksgiving in her heart.

Next morning when she let the dog out, the air was dense and heavy, the temperature was warmer, and the snow was close to becoming sloppy.

Damaris called for Hurit, who came towards her from the woods' edge.

She was so focused on watching the dog contend with the snow that she did not notice the man until he was nearly in front of her.

"Who are you?" a young man's voice startled her.

He was dressed in leather leggings and moccasins. He had a linen shirt with long sleeves. His long, dark scalp lock was adorned by split turkey tail feathers tied in a cluster that hung down to the right side of his youthful face. His copper cheeks were flushed and he was not wearing war paint. In the morning light, she could see the snowshoe tracks that led to where he stood. From the track marks she could tell that he had just arrived from the west.

Damaris was about to introduce herself when Hurit made her way to the handsome young man right as he was about to step out of his snowshoes. Hurit jumped up with both feet to his chest and knocked him over. Her tail wagged wildly and he laughed and rubbed her shoulders. The dog licked his face. They obviously knew each other.

When he turned toward Damaris, he brought the flat of his hand up to his chest. "Owaneco, my name."

Damaris blushed at being caught staring at Owaneco. "Uh, I'm Damaris Cooke." She found herself compelled to say, "I see you have come from west of here." She pointed in the direction of the snowshoe tracks.

Owaneco stepped over to the pung. "This yours?" He inspected it closely. "You make this?" His eyes twinkled as the corners of his mouth began to curl.

Damaris could hardly believe that this young person could remind her so much of Jacob's sense of humor. "No," she smiled. "It is on loan from Reverend Eliot. The Natick men built the pung. Amie and I like it very much. It has served us well so far."

Owaneco nodded politely, went inside, and disappeared.

Chapter Twenty-Nine

❦Norwich❦

Damaris

Norwich was only a few miles away. They found Reverend Fitch in his office at the Congregational Church, just as John Eliot said.

His office was not a big room in comparison to the overall size of the church and sanctuary.

The building was much larger than the simple meetinghouse in Namasket or even the newly built, white church in Plymouth. The town of Norwich was a much larger village than Damaris had expected.

Amie and Damaris settled in the seats to the left, facing the sturdy desk where the heavy-set, middle-aged Reverend Fitch was seated. He was dressed in dark clothes with a high, white collar that gave him the appearance of importance. On the reverend's right sat Thomas Leffingwell and Oweneco, and on the left, Amie and Damaris were joined by Mary Uncas Leffingwell.

Damaris opened the leather pouch with the wampum belts and important papers but was interrupted by a quick knock on the door. Without waiting, Uncas entered and joined the men to the right of the reverend.

Uncas, a powerful presence in the room, wore a bright blue shirt with a floral print, like no fabric made in the Americas. It would have come to him directly through trade with the English. He wore many silver earrings in both of his ears. The ear wheels, an array of balls and cones mixed with hoops, hung heavy from holes along the edge of his ears and lobes. He also wore a fair amount of woven wampum over his shoulder and silver pieces on his shirt. His headdress was much the same as what his son Oweneco wore, and he, too, wore no war paint.

Before anyone had the chance to speak, another knock was heard, but whoever was on the other side did not let themselves in as Uncas had done. Thomas rose and opened the door. A small group of Nipmucks entered, leaving Mary, Amie, and Damaris to cram closer in order to make room. The small group appeared as though they had been on the move and did not have time to make themselves as presentable as they might have liked.

From the moment they arrived, the Nipmucks gathered around Uncas and Oweneco and spoke to them in an Algonquin dialect that Damaris struggled to understand.

The Nipmucks had come to Uncas for some form of help.

Before the Nipmuck people left, Reverend Fitch prayed with them. Damaris watched the rag-tag group, who had entered in a fluster, leave calmly, thanking Uncas and Reverend Fitch graciously.

Their own personal meeting with Reverend Fitch went well for Amie, in that Uncas and Oweneco agreed to allow Amie to join them on the trek up to Schaghticoke with the Nipmuck and a Jesuit Father named Drusllette, who they said was a friend of John Eliot. The plan was for Amie to blend in with the party of Nipmuck. She and others were to become part of a new inter-tribal community that would absorb the Christian praying Indians. If all went well, they would be known by the name Schaghticoke, meaning,

"People Of The Mingling Waters." They would settle where the Tomahanock and the Hoosic rivers came together.

Instead of sending Damaris with the Leffingwells to Uncas's village, Reverend Fitch began to make plans for her safe return to Massachusetts Bay. He made it clear that since she was not an Indian, she was expected to spend the night at the Fitch manse.

The time was near for parting.

Damaris and Amie embraced for a long time. They stepped back, eyes locked. They saw into each other's souls, exchanging such thoughts as no words could express. Only their hearts could speak.

Then as Uncas, Oweneco, Thomas, Mary, and Amie were filing out of the office, Damaris turned her attention to the reverend. "Please, sir, if you will forgive me for asking, it is a kind and generous offer you have made for me to stay at your fine home, but if it would be alright with you, I want to spend as much time with Amie as I am able before she has to leave."

He was agreeable to that.

The next day Damaris watched the Nipmucks, Uncas, and Oweneco lower themselves into dugout canoes and paddle upriver. She stood on the shore with the Leffingwells and Reverend Fitch and watched until the small armada that carried her friend Amie disappeared from view.

Her mission had been accomplished.

Chapter Thirty

Ruth's Precious Discovery

Excerpt from the writings of Damaris Cooke,
1677 Massachusetts.

I am finding it difficult to express in words
how I felt that day when I watched my dear friend
Amie get into the canoe that would take her to
Schaghticoke. All I can say is that my heart hurt,
but it was good to know she would be safe.

The Leffingwells were so kind as to see me safely
back to the Inn at Massachusetts Bay.

Soon after, Mother Bond died, and Mary sent
word that Ruth and I should come to live with her
in Plymouth.

Damaris

Namasket was halfway between the Bay Colony and Plymouth, and Damaris was more than ready to get on the move. "What is taking John Rickard so long to return from the livery?" Damaris asked Mary.

Mary's eyes twinkled and her mouth pulled tight like it always did when she was hiding something, then she broke into a full smile when her husband appeared with the horse.

"Barge!" Damaris exclaimed. All frustration about getting a late start disappeared as she ran to greet the dappled mare that had belonged to Jacob.

"I recognized Jacob's horse at one of the camps," John explained. "I had to trade more than she's worth to get them to let her go."

Damaris laid her head on the horse's thick neck and reached her arm underneath and patted the other side. "Thank you very much, John. Having Barge back makes me feel like a part of Jacob has returned to comfort me."

"Me, too," Ruth said as she joined her mother in welcoming the horse.

After getting a late start from the Bay Colony, John Rickard decided to make camp earlier than Damaris would have wished. She was eager for the trip to be over. They slept in a meadow overnight.

The next day, Damaris followed behind Ruth, who insisted on leading the horse. Ahead were Mary and John. The grandchildren were waiting with Betty in Plymouth.

Damaris soaked up the warm rays of the sun in the clear blue eastern sky. A fresh scent, diffused from green leaves after the cleansing rain, filled her nostrils, and a gentle breeze brought welcome warmth that quickly dried her overdress. She smiled up at God, thankful she and her family were on their way toward Plymouth.

Ruth reached back and passed the lead rope for Barge. "Mother, can you take him for a while? My hand is sore."

Damaris took the lead from Ruth's soft, white hand and found herself eye level with the girl's chest. In that moment she realized that Ruth's breasts filled the bodice of the fine dress Sara Bond had insisted she take. Damaris looked up and noticed her hair. It, too, had far more volume than she remembered. The thickness of it reminded her of Jacob.

"I'm thankful to God for the Bonds. They took such good care of you," Damaris said from her place behind. The trek gave her time to reflect and ready herself for the future. "The Lord will see me through what is to come," she thought.

Suddenly, melancholy began to bubble up as it did from time to time since Jacob's passing. She patted the nose of Jacob's gentle old horse, and they trod together along the well-worn footpath. "Traveling with Amie, I had a mission and a purpose." She patted Barge. "It helped keep my mind off of living without Jacob."

After a time, Damaris walked a little faster until she caught up with Ruth. "The first time I was on this ancient trail I was with your grandfather," she said.

Ruth slowed and turned her ear toward her mother.

"Your grandfather, Stephen, measured the depth of the trail and found that it was sixteen inches. Just think about how many feet have traveled here." Damaris stopped and bent down to check the wall of the beaten path. "This earthen trail has worn down at least two more inches since I was a young girl traveling on it with my father."

Ruth didn't comment; instead, she smiled.

Bits and pieces of conversations were drifting Damaris's way. "...add on a room." "Mr. Tinkham...making a cradle." The drone of their voices lulled Damaris into thoughts about family. The word "cradle" sparked her attention. She listened to what they were talking about and felt the forepart of her body tingle mysteriously with anticipation of holding a newborn babe. It would be sometime in the next five months. "If it is a boy I want to call him Jacob," Mary said.

The thought of Mary's pregnancy helped ease her heart. She closed her eyes for a moment and began to imagine herself drawing the future little baby up, feeling the little one's body warmth, and hearing sweet infant coos.

"We are going to build onto the house so that you will have a room of your very own," Mary said, turning her head in her mother's direction. "No more cabins for you. It will be a wonderful room." She emphasized the word room and engaged her big brown eyes before saying, "Mother, you just wait and see."

Damaris kept any thoughts about wanting to go back to the simple life to herself. With Jacob gone, she knew that she would not be able go back to log and chink walls and oiled paper windows. That life was gone forever, but she would tell the story. God willing, it would be her winter project.

After they had traveled as far as Namasket, they stopped for a rest and to enjoy some of the food Mary had packed.

Damaris examined the grounds where she had once lived. There were remnants of their lives left scattered here and there. Some broken pottery, partly burned chunks of this and that such as a half-burned pack basket and the metal rings from what had once been a barrel. She walked about and neared the charred remains of the cabins. She kicked at an old broken rail and stirred up dust and soot. Had it been hers? She didn't know.

Suddenly she heard Ruth's voice. "Mother, come see what I found. You won't believe it."

Damaris followed Ruth's voice into a small wooded area near where her cabin had been. That is when she saw the rocker. Jacob's chair was lying on its side where it must have landed, having been tossed there during the raid. When she squatted down to check it out, she found that it had escaped the fire and only been damaged in two places. The top right had a crack in it and one of the spindles was broken in half.

She did not know if she should laugh or cry at the sight of it. She looked at Ruth. "I think we can fix it. Don't you?"

Ruth helped her mother untangle some of the weeds to get her father's rocker out, and in the process she soiled the silk dress with a green smudge. Damaris watched it happen. "Oh, no. Your beautiful dress is ruined."

Ruth went back to the task and undid the last of the vines. "This chair is all we have left of our home. It is worth much more than a dress."

After the family had enjoyed Mary's lunch, they decided to make the push to go all the way on to Plymouth and camp only if they had to.

Damaris insisted on carrying the chair herself even though sometimes it dug into her back and shoulders. The monotony as she trudged along caused her to think about how she would find a special place in her room for Jacob's chair.

Damaris thought it might even be nice to have a chest of drawers to put clothes in, once she acquired some much-needed apparel. She sensed concentrated smoke from the blacksmith fires, muck, mud, and the sweet aroma of baking bread before she could see Plymouth. She paused, set the chair down on the ridge where she and Amie once played, sat down in it, and prayed, "Lord, one thing for sure I really desire is to have a writing desk and a quality quill, for I have much I want to say."

Chapter Thirty-One

~A Letter from Amie~

Damaris

Damaris moved Jacob's rocker and a large wooden bowl from Mary's house outside into the warmth of the sun, where she set herself to the task of popping peas from their pods into her bowl.

"Whoa."

She watched the horse and wagon stop across the way. The man with the reins stayed seated while a young man wearing English trousers and a plain linen shirt hopped down and headed toward her.

"Oweneco!" Damaris exclaimed and steadied her bowl. "How are you?" The sight of Oweneco caused a rush of mental images to flash across her mind. He reminded her of Reverend Fitch and the Leffingwells, and of Amie. The last time she had seen him was the day Amie left for Schaghticoke. She smiled. "How are you? Did the trip go well? Is Schaghticoke a good place?" Oweneco's face went blank. "I'm sorry," Damaris said. "I'm sorry for talking so fast."

Oweneco dropped his head and reached into his pocket. "This for you."

Damaris set the bowl of peas aside to take the bundle. The letter from Amie was neatly tied with a bright blue ribbon. She gently placed it on her lap. "Can you stay to dinner with us?"

Oweneco pointed toward the horse and wagon across the way. "He waits for me." Then he fumbled around and pulled out another small bundle and handed it to Damaris. "This for Amie's daughter. You give to her, yes?"

"Yes." Damaris lifted Betty's letter, neatly tied with a yellow ribbon, up to her nose, closed her eyes, and breathed in. It smelled of wood fire, sweat, and wilderness. Her eyes opened wide as she leaned toward the young man and spoke slowly. "Amie? Is she well?"

Oweneco tipped his head in the direction of Damaris's hands that were covering the bundles. "Look there. Hands hold answer." Then his face lit up and his eyes twinkled the way Jacob's would. "The news is good."

Damaris looked down at the letter and back up only to see Oweneco turning to leave. "Say hello to your father and the Leffingwells for me."

"I will."

Just then the door opened and it was Mary. "Who was that?"

Damaris felt a little giddy in the moment. "The young man that I told you about who reminds me of your father. He brought letters from Amie. This one is for Betty."

Mary took the letter and went back into the house to find Betty.

Damaris breathed deeply, rocked the chair, and absorbed the sun's rays before she slowly pulled on the blue ribbon and began to read her letter from Amie.

Schaghticoke
1676
My Dear Friend Damaris,
*　　I hope that this letter finds you faring well. I wrote to Betty telling her that the land Tispiquin*

gave to her and Sassamon is hers. All she would need to do is go see the clerk there in Plymouth to find that I registered it as Betty's Neck. If she goes back there, her cabin should still stand. She could send word to me when she thinks it safe for me to return.

You need not worry about me, because I plan to return to Namasket in the coming year.

Schaghticoke is a beautiful place between the Hoosic and Tomahanock rivers. It is a place where people from different tribes have agreed to live in peace together and I have made many new friends among the citizenry here.

This is a place established for trading. People come and go with their goods. I have not seen so many furs as that come through here. There are wool blankets and textiles of every kind in the trading post.

Thanks to John Eliot, I am able to teach people how to read and write. I also have learned to make shirts for sale in the trading post. I'm glad we learned both English and Algonquin, but now I wish I had learned French and Mohawk. I am starting to pick up a few words they speak. It will take time. The French traders don't come here all that much but I still would like to understand what they say. A secret: there is a Frenchman that I like to see come here. His eyes light up when he talks with the clerk at the post. I like the way he smiles. I wish to know what he is saying.

On our way here, a runner came to us with the word that my brother had failed to get the

Mohawk to join him against the English and that Philip was killed on his return.

Now that King Philip is no more, people from many tribes and countries have agreed to live in peace together in order to trade. The remnants of praying towns have been welcomed here. I am now a member of the Schaghticoke lodge.

I shall do my best to describe what took place here, February last. I have never seen anything like the immense thanksgiving gathering. There was an unusual thaw that made it possible for more remnant bands of fugitive Christians to attend.

I sat back behind the council with the Abenaki women and children, but from where we sat, I could see and hear most everything that happened. The women we sat near were Mohawk who came down from the north. In front of us, seated in circles, in accordance to their position, were at least one thousand warriors from the Mohawks, Abenakis, Hoosacs, Mahicansacs, Pequots, Narragansetts, Wampanoags, Pennacooks, Lenni-Lenapes, and Onondagas assembled to hold the conference of peace with Governor Andros. Also behind us, surrounding the circle, were uniformed militia of Governor Andros's staff.

It was explained to me that a decision had been made and there was going to happen an assemblage of friendship. The symbol would be the planting of a sapling oak.

We watched them dig the hole and plant the oak. Governor Andros poured pure river water over the seedling from a horn goblet to bless the earth for the tree. He called it the Witenagemot tree of peace.

Soquan stood, and spoke a Great Thanksgiving Prayer where he returned thanks to the Creator for everything under the earth, such as the worms that aerate the soil. He gave thanks for human beings, those who had gone before us, and those yet unborn. He gave thanks for the two-legged and four-legged who walk upon the earth, and the winged of the air, the three sisters, and medicine plants. He gave thanks for all these things that sustain human beings. Then he thanked the Creator for the moon, the stars, the prophets, and, above all, he thanked the Creator of all things for His very being with hopes this ceremony was pleasing to Him.

Then Uncas, Aepjen, Soquan, Maquan, Wanalancet, and Gray-Lock stepped to the center. Aepjen lifted his hand high in the air, holding up the magnificent quill-adorned Mno-ti (bag of peace) of the Abenakis Nation. It held belts of wampum and a calumet of peace. After the pipe ceremony, Kryn of the Mohawk broke the strings of his bow, wiped the blood off his hatchet, and buried the implements of war beneath the roots of the tree, saying, "Great Manitou, cleanse our beds and scatter all dark clouds."

Jesuit Father Drusllette, the one who traveled with me here, and Fathers Bruyas and Boniface of the Mohawk missions, and the Dutch Dominies, Sachacts, and Van Rensselear of Fort Orange offered prayers and sang anthems during the closing ceremony of the passing of the Calumet (pipe of peace) around the circles. All who were present were obliged to partake of at least a whiff of the smoke. Then there was an exchange of many gifts among those who participated.

After Soquan pronounced the benediction, a big dance ensued.

I will never forget what I had the honor to witness on that day. My description is but a small measure of what took place here.

I pray the peace will last.

Please send me a letter soon with the news of Plymouth, and know that you are forever in my heart, dear friend.

May the Lord bless you, Damaris.

Amie

Damaris folded each page of her precious letter carefully, tied them back together with the blue ribbon, and lifted the bundle to her heart with thanksgiving to God.

The Peace that was established in 1676 at Old Schaghticoke lasted almost a hundred years. It ended with the onset of the Revolutionary War.

THE END

❧Bibliography❧

History Of The Town Of Middleboro, Massachusetts (1906)
by Thomas Weston
Kessinger Legacy Reprints
This is the book that first sparked Praying Town. I was looking up Jacob and Damaris Cooke and found that they lived in Middleborough, Massachusetts. I found the above book and read this:

> "EARLY SETTLERS BEFORE KING PHILIP'S WAR.... The settlement of Middleboro was unlike that of other places, in that these men supposed that the town was to be occupied in common with the aborigines, who were then the owners of much of the land."

The book gave a short description of that simple lifestyle of hewn log homes with oil-paper windows and wooden latches. Her people dressed in linsey-woolsey and leather breeches they tanned from bear, deer, etc. Then the book moved on to its development after King Philip's War to the present day of its publication in 1906. That is when I began my quest to find out why they lived in harmony. What was going on? So then, I found a book titled:

The Times of Their Lives: Life, Love, and Death in Plymouth Colony
By James Deetz and Patricia Scott Deetz
This book's subject matter was a fascinating read about little-known details of Plymouth Colony, but for the most

part predated the latter 1700s. However, it did make a reference to the John Sassamon trial. That led me to:

Igniting King Philip's War: The John Sassamon Murder Trial
by Yasuhide Kawashima

I referred to this book to learn about the trial and found that Yasuhide Kawashima had created a timeline, which I loved and referred to many times. In the glossary, the word Schaghticoke caught my eye (the very town where I grew up; the site of the Peace Tree my dad was always talking about.) Yasuhide Kawashima called it a missionary town in New York. He also gave the names of the six sage Indians who served on the Sassamon trial's jury.

The other book I relied on for detailed information about King Philip's War was:

The Name of War: King Philip's War and the Origins of American Identity
by Jill Lepore

This book told about John Eliot, the praying towns, and the translation of the Bible into the Algonquin language. She also gave details of the suffering that happened on Deer Island and a description of what the peace medal looked like.

Speaking of peace:

The Hoosic Valley: Its Legends and Its History
by Grace Greylock Niles

Here I found a detailed description of the Peace Council that took place at Schaghticoke.

My inspiration for Thomas Leffingwell's wife being Uncas's daughter came from research on the internet for her genealogy.

"Thomas Leffingwell's Indian Wife" from Genealogy.com
http://www.genealogy.com/forum/surnames/topics/leffingwell/271/
by Melissa Marrero

Melissa concluded that most facts pointed to Mary being of native descent.

Last but not least is the Holy Bible I chose to use for the wedding, John Eliot's Algonquin version:

MAMUSSE
WUNNEETUPANATATAMWE
UP BIBLUM GOD
NANEESWE
NUKKONE TESTAMENT
KAH WON
WUSKU TESTAMENT
John Eliot
1663

And for translation:

HOLY BIBLE
Authorized King James Version

Photo courtesy of
First Light Photography
Puyallup, WA

❧About the Author❧

G awenase is a Christian whose mother was full-blood Danish. Her father's deep Algonquin and Colonial roots include a Civil war Congressional Medal of Honor recipient, George Washington's drummer boy, six Mayflower passengers, and two connections to Uncas of the Mohegan, as well as original families of Vermont, Connecticut, Massachusetts, New York, and New Hampshire. She is, therefore, a direct descendant of those who came over on the Mayflower and of those who greeted them with mixed reaction.

She grew up in the village of Schaghticoke in upstate New York. As a young girl, she became active on the pow-wow trail. She was given the name "Gawenase" in midwinter of 1969 and was adopted Seneca. She is a member of the Coos Cowasuck Band of the Pennacook Abenaki People of the White Pine.

She studied art under Tom Two Arrows, Onondaga/Delaware, who created his particular style of Indian Art back in the 1940s. Some of her paintings and craft works are owned by the United States Department of the Interior Indian Arts and Crafts Board, as well as in private collections.

She worked as a park interpreter for the United States Department of the Interior; Historical Parks at Saratoga, NY; The Helderburg Workshop, Guilderland, NY; and was a teaching assistant for adult classes at Albany State University.

On the powwow trail, after moving to the West Coast, she connected with other displaced Eastern Woodland families who have made an earnest effort to keep the Woodland traditions alive.

In Eastern Woodland Impressions, she and her friend Monika DeNasha do intricate bead work. Their motto is "Preserving the past in the present for the future."

She lives with her husband, Roger, on a farm near Puget Sound, and at powwow these days, she dances in the women's Golden Age.

97951990R00159

Made in the USA
Columbia, SC
15 June 2018